A LISTING

OF THE WORKS OF

ROBERT NATHAN

WILL BE FOUND AT THE END

OF THIS VOLUME

THE DEVIL
WITH LOVE

THE DEVIL
with LOVE

BY

ROBERT NATHAN

NEW YORK

Alfred · A · Knopf

1963

L. C. catalog card number: 63-11048

THIS IS A BORZOI BOOK
PUBLISHED BY ALFRED A. KNOPF, INC.

FIRST EDITION

For Minnie

FOR SURELY, *Spirit is of another Dimension, being bound neither by Space nor Time. Yet its recognizance is in the Mind, which is of the present, being composed of organic matter, and therefor mortal. Thought alone overskips the boundaries of Past and Future, conceives of the Soul, and races after Eternity; only that power of the mind which we call Imagination can touch, for a moment, the rim of that Mystery, that Glory, which is beyond our understanding.*

(*From* The Mysterium Magnum
*of Bernard of Treves,
translated by Ben Ray Redman*)

THE STRENGTH *of religion lies not in the unquestionable answer, but in the unanswerable question.*

(*Alexander Courage:
"Principles of Belief"*)

THE DEVIL
WITH LOVE

CHAPTER 1

The sound of the Angelus bell floated in the air above the little town of Parish between the hills and the sea. Faint and hollow it drifted above the pines and the boulders which covered the shore and the cliffs on which the town nestled like a bird, and was carried by the sea-wind inland to the hill-sheltered valleys and the faraway mountains.

Like the town, the Catholic church in Parish was small, and its pastor, Father Deener, had to do without the services of a curate. But this did not keep him from taking a generous view of the universe. He saw it as something beyond his comprehension, and the more mysterious it appeared, the more unripe and ignorant he knew himself to be. He was filled with awe at the richness of life, in which he sensed a complicated and powerful design; but he was convinced that man was not supposed to understand it. This did not depress him: on the contrary, it filled him with joy because he realized that if he were expected to know everything, he would have to insist like the Russian astronaut that God did not exist because he hadn't seen Him.

It made him happy to believe that everything was possible, to open his heart to the miracles of the past as well as the explorations of the present. He was aware of the great advances in science; but just the same, when someone announced that the creation of the universe had been an accident, he felt obliged to ask: an accident to what?

In short, he was humble, but obstinate; out of all the possibilities, out of all the faces of God, he had chosen the one which appealed to him the most. He believed in the saints and the angels, and in Holy Writ, including both the Old Testament and the New; he believed it all, because, as he said, he couldn't see any reason not to. God either was, or He wasn't; in a mystery of such magnitude it seemed a waste of time to argue over trifles.

Now, in the evening, he walked with his friend Miss Mary Sebastian in his garden beneath the sea-pines, and smelled the fragrance of roses and honeysuckle. Below him the sea foamed among the rocks, sending up a breath of cold air; and he saw above him the fading sky where, as a child, he had imagined God to be.

Mary Sebastian was the Parish postmaster; or perhaps it would be better to say that she was the town's postmistress. She was a quiet woman of thirty-nine, neither plain nor pretty, long-legged, small-breasted, innocent, and calm. She had grown up in Parish, and she had been Father Deener's friend ever since she could remember. These evening visits to the priest's little garden were as much a part of her everyday life as opening the post office in the morning.

Sometimes they walked in silence; or they discussed town affairs, or the mysteries of the universe. A jet plane, floating through the evening air, winked its red and green lights above them, already far ahead of its own thunder. In the east the sky had darkened, but above the hills to the north a faint corona of light spread its pale glow between the darker blue of the zenith and the somber mass of earth. To the west, out across the shadowy sea, the sky was green as melon rind. Father Deener remarked pensively:

"When I was a child, it was the evening express, clanking and sighing its way across the prairies, and lighted up like a palace. Since then, man has extended himself into the empty air; and young people are already going down into the sea among the kelp, the corals, and the fish. Perhaps we are returning to the elements from which we came, air and water."

"We were fish to begin with," said Miss Sebastian. "The human embryo has gills in its early stages. I read that in Dr. Fleming's office once, in a magazine."

"That only makes everything more mysterious," said Father Deener. "There was a moment, apparently, when the Creator . . ."

He stopped and cleared his throat in embarrassment. "Just the same," he said obstinately, "I like to think that God made man in His own image, no matter how many doubts may have occurred to Him along the way."

"Me, too," agreed Miss Sebastian. "I always see God as a fatherly man with a beard." She smiled gaily, and gave a hop to avoid stepping on a toad on the path. "But what does the Devil look like?" she asked.

"Who knows?" Father Deener replied. "Martin Luther saw him, and threw an inkpot at his head. The result was unexpected: it gave rise to the Protestant Church. He appeared to scores of men and women during the Middle Ages, and throughout the Reformation; in fact, it was during the Reformation that the busiest traffic in souls may be said to have taken place."

Miss Sebastian made a face. "Do you believe that the Devil buys souls?" she asked.

Father Deener lifted his hands in a gesture of helplessness. "My dear child," he said, "who can define Infinity? Or describe Eternity? In those further, mysterious dimensions, what unbelievable things are not possible! Let us simply say that we do not know, and let it go at that."

But he was interested in the details of his parish, for which he had worked so many years. "They say there's to be a road put in past the McHenry house," said Miss Sebastian, who in addition to the newspaper brought him the town gossip every evening. "It's to cost over ten thousand dollars."

"Ah," said Father Deener with satisfaction. Thomas McHenry was one of his own parishioners, a man who made his contributions to the Church; and he was pleased to think of his good fortune. "I haven't seen Thomas lately," he remarked. "How has he been feeling? The last time I saw him, I thought he looked a little peaked."

Miss Sebastian, who usually knew where people were, replied:

"He's gone to Rockford, on some business thing."

"Did he take his son with him again?"

He was informed that both Mr. McHenry and his young son had left Parish the day before. With a sinking heart, he inquired:

"And Mrs. McHenry?"

The postmistress was silent for a moment, gazing up at the heavens which had turned dark with the coming night. "Um," she said at last, uncertainly.

"I see," said the priest. "Is it the drink?"

"Yes," said Mary unwillingly.

Father Deener sighed. "Well," he said, "you'd better not tell me about it."

But he knew he'd have to go see Mrs. McHenry sooner or later, and he dreaded it. What could he say to her? She too had her problems.

As Father Deener prepared for bed that night, he wondered how much Thomas McHenry knew about what went on during those absences from home when he took his eight-year-old son with him to a business convention or on a fishing trip. Or did he, perhaps, take the boy in order to get him out of the house, recognizing the signs, knowing what was coming—the week-long drinking bout that would culminate in forty-eight sodden hours?

Pulling his nightgown down over his head, the old priest sighed wearily. Why am I the one, he thought, chosen to deliver this unhappy woman from her troubles? Couldn't the Lord have thought of a more likely person?

Kneeling before the Crucifix which hung on the wall above his bed, Father Deener asked for help. "I am only a man," he said. "Do not ask me to do this all by myself."

Thus, long ago, the monk Paphnutius asked God to help him convert the courtesan Thaïs. But Paphnutius lived in a simpler age, when the sun moved around the earth, and demons appeared in the form of small animals and made conversation. Paphnutius saw the constellations above his head and thought that they were the windows of Heaven, from which at any moment an angel might descend with advice and consolation.

"After all, Lord," said Father Deener humbly, "You were nearer then."

A few days later a black door opened in the night-blue sky and something came through. There was a sudden piercing cold which lasted no more than a moment; and the church bell rang once of its own accord and then was still. The sound was so faint that Father Deener wasn't even sure he'd heard it.

CHAPTER 2

Alfred Sneeden, who did repairs to radios, electric clocks, and television sets, was seated in the dark, on the damp, rocky ground of the hill above the Milhouser house, watching the little square of yellow-golden light which, he had reason to believe, marked the window of Gladys Milhouser's bedroom. The blind was drawn, but occasionally a vague shape passed like a shadow behind the windowshade.

Gladys was the daughter of Leo Milhouser, who owned the service station, the liquor store, and the bowling alley. She was a pretty girl of seventeen, with a mop of golden hair which she sprayed every day with Herpal's Beauty Spray, in order to make it swing from side to side the way people's hair did on television . . . those young beauties with their lustrous, wavy hair, gazing out of the screen at her. She had been voted Home-Coming Queen of Parish High School for the year just passed; she had been one of the cheer leaders and a member of the girls' basketball team. She loved sodas, jukeboxes, dancing, riding in a convertible with the top down, and the stories of J. D. Salinger. She had been obliged to read Shakespeare in her sophomore year, but she preferred Salinger.

To Alfred Sneeden, nearing middle age, Gladys Milhouser was the most beautiful thing he had ever seen. In his waking dreams he imagined her as his own—not as Mrs. Sneeden, for such an introduction of reality into his fantasy would have

destroyed it. Rather, he saw himself with Gladys
resting ambiguously on his bosom, innocent, grateful, melting with love, and swimming in tender
tears.

In his untidy bedroom over his shop with its
coils and wires, dilapidated radios, TV tubes, and
bits of electrical equipment, he kept a picture of
her clipped from the county newspaper. She was
smiling at the photographer, who had posed her in
her Home-Coming gown, and she was holding a
sheaf of flowers; but it seemed to Alfred that she
was smiling at him. And as he ate his supper of
frankfurters and beans or a canned soup, he imagined that she spoke to him. What she said was
friendly and comforting; all it lacked was words.

He had actually had a conversation with her
once. It was when he had been called in to repair
the television set in Mr. Milhouser's home: he had
asked her what was wrong with it, and she had
told him. "It's the thingummy," she had said, "that
doesn't work."

He saw her now and then, always with other young people, friends and classmates, sitting at the drugstore soda fountain, talking and laughing, driving down the main street in somebody's old car with no top, her golden hair swinging from side to side; at the beach in summer, sprawled on the sand, or striking out through the surf with her surfboard, and then coming in on the rollers, erect and supple, slicing down across the green water, or tossed in a smother of foam. It was then that his heart beat too fast, and he found himself holding his breath, while his whole body ached with misery and longing.

Everyone has some illusion about himself, however secret and humble. He had almost no hope that she would ever notice him, but, in his dreams, she was immediately attracted to him. When he passed her on the street all he could manage was a frightened grin, to which she responded with indifference, if, indeed, she noticed it at all.

He knew of no way to make her aware of him.

And in all probability nothing would have happened if Father Deener hadn't gone to pay his call on Delia McHenry on the very day that Alfred Sneeden was at the McHenry house, putting new tubes in the big radio in the living room.

Father Deener and Mrs. McHenry were seated in the dining room, behind closed doors; but Alfred could hear bits of their conversation; at least, he could hear the priest, while Mrs. McHenry seemed inclined to mumble. She had been drinking, but it was still early in the day, and she carried herself with a certain dignity, though she seemed to give way at times to a falling off of the spirit.

"It's when Tom—Mr. McHenry—goes off on those long trips," she was saying tearfully, and then something about his taking the boy.

"Ah," said Father Deener, "but does it begin before or after?"

Mrs. McHenry's answer was inaudible. "Now then, my dear," said Father Deener gently, "that's not the whole of it."

"Well, no—it isn't," she conceded. "There's this thing comes over me . . . like it was just waiting for the moment . . ."

"I've no doubt of it," said Father Deener. "The Serpent himself was lurking in the Garden, waiting . . ."

"It's not so much out-of-doors, as in," said Delia. "It's the emptiness."

"Then go out-of-doors," said Father Deener, "and work in the flower beds."

There was some further inaudible response from Mrs. McHenry, but Alfred, listening with all his ears, gathered that she didn't like gardening.

For a while the conversation seemed to have something to do with roses, and Alfred lost interest. But then he suddenly heard the priest exclaim in firm tones:

"Satan comes when he is called!"

And he went on to explain that the Devil never sleeps. "You must never summon him," he declared, "for he will come; and he will demand something in return."

She must have asked him what, for he replied:

"Your immortal soul."

And he went on to tell Mrs. McHenry the story of Faust, who summoned Mephistopheles and asked for the gift of youth, and for the young and innocent Marguerite, for whom he was willing to sign away his soul. "This Faust," said Father Deener, "made the obvious mistake of thinking that his soul was old, weary, bent, and rheumatic as he was—not realizing that the soul is incorruptible.

"That is," he added a trifle uncertainly, "after it has been cleansed of original sin."

This was always a ticklish point with Father Deener, who preferred to think that man, born into the world in the image of his Maker, was born innocent.

The next day, walking as usual in his garden at evening, the priest said to his friend the postmistress:

"I am convinced that the Church is wrong on this point."

Miss Sebastian was surprised. "I thought you enjoyed your ignorance," she said. "How can you be convinced of anything like that?"

Father Deener bowed his head in shame. "You are right," he said humbly. "I ought to know better."

And he resumed his pacing of the garden, his hands clasped behind his back. The sweet air of evening with its fragrance of earth and flowers flowed about him, but he scarcely noticed it. There it is again, he thought: the sin of pride. And what is more, I am guilty of contradicting myself.

Why should I think I have found the answer to questions which have puzzled the world for thousands of years?

"Do you know anyone in Parish named Marguerite?" asked Miss Sebastian.

"Marguerite?" said Father Deener, rousing himself. "Marguerite who?"

The postmistress explained that Mr. Sneeden had come into the post office that afternoon and had asked her if she knew Marguerite. "Or perhaps it was 'about' Marguerite," she said. "I don't know. I thought it strange."

Father Deener stroked his chin absent-mindedly. "Sneeden," he said slowly; "I think I've seen the man. Is he a Catholic?"

"I don't know," said Miss Sebastian. "I think so. But all he said was, did I know Marguerite?"

"Maybe she's a relative," said Father Deener. "Would the post office know where to reach her?"

"Marguerite who, for goodness' sakes?"

"Sneeden, I suppose," said Father Deener, and resumed his pacing.

In the dark, on his hill above the Milhouser mansion, Alfred felt the damp earth under him, and shivered. The little square of Gladys' window shone in the garden below, and as he watched with his heart in his throat, the shade was suddenly lifted and Gladys herself appeared framed in the lamplight. She was wearing a frilly cotton nightgown; as a matter of fact, he had seen more of her on the beach, but never in such a secret and guilty way, or with such a sense of the forbidden, and the delicious. His hands were clenched at his sides, he arched forward, his eyes, his very soul, seemed to be leaving his body, straining toward her through the dark.

She leaned for a moment on the window sill, gazing out at the night; she seemed to sigh, and wrapped a curl of hair around one finger. Then she drew back into the room, and in a minute or two the light went out, leaving the night blacker than before.

Alfred found himself trembling. He wanted her so much; he thought that he would give anything in the world for her. He knew that he was no fit match for her, that he was too old; he longed to be like those boys who played with her on the beach, who danced with her at school dances, took her driving in their cars with the top down. . . . He envied them with all his heart, he was jealous of their right to be with her. . . .

He'd give anything in the world to be young,

like them. What was that story about a man who'd wanted a girl so much that he'd sold his soul to the Devil? Her name was Marguerite; he'd forgotten the man's name. He wouldn't mind doing it himself, he thought, for a girl like Gladys. She could have everything he had; she could have anything he had in the world.

The darkness around him seemed unusually silent; even the crickets were quiet. The night lay still, waiting; as he, too, waited; and the longing in his heart seemed to swell until it seemed as though it would burst. A man couldn't live like that, he thought, to want something so much, and not to have it.

He was beginning to feel queer, too. He scrambled awkwardly to his feet, stiff and cramped from sitting so long on the ground. "All right," he said with bravado, and what he thought was a mocking smile: "you, out there—

"You think you can make me young again? Anything I've got, you can have. My soul, for that girl."

If he expected an answer, he was disappointed. The night lay around him silent as before; and Gladys' window remained dark and unlighted below.

But it was then that the door opened in the sky, and the thing came through. It was as though an icy wind blew suddenly there on the hill.

Alfred went home and got into bed, with a woolen sock wrapped around his throat. He thought he might have caught a cold.

CHAPTER 3

Lucifer, the great Archangel, stood in awful majesty upon the highest pinnacle of Hell. The fallen Seraph, folded in his immense wings as in a cloak of darkness, gazed with somber eyes at the demons ranged around him, who returned his look with apprehension. His expression, naturally lofty and severe, was even more critical than usual.

Below him, in Limbo, waited the uneasy souls

of the unbaptized and unredeemed: there, for the first time, ancient man saw his descendants. There the Mousterian and the Aurignacian confronted each other, and the Neanderthal gazed in awe at the artist of the cave-paintings of the Dordogne. Arrayed in terrible armor the hosts of the Sumerians, Egyptians, Chaldeans, Persians, Greeks, Scythians, Parthians, and early Romans maneuvered for advantage, while the armies of Attila and Genghis Khan moved like locusts across the empty plain.

They could be forgiven because they had never known any better. The damned were still further down, in pits of molten fire—in particular those heretics who had rebelled against Mother Church. Among them were the Albigensians and the Cathars; the Cathars in particular were indignant at what had happened to them.

In the very lowest pits of all were thrown those souls who had sinned against the Devil himself, by attempting to outdo him in evil. Here were to be found such characters as the Marquis de Sade, Bluebeard, and Dr. Crippen. However, his greatest indignation was reserved for those who denied God. "It is all very well to defy Him, as I do," he declared, "but it's quite another thing to deny His existence! To do so is to deny my own—for where would I be without that great and shining Adversary?"

"I believe that you love Him!" exclaimed Beelzebub in surprise.

Lucifer made a gesture of impatience. "I don't love Him," he said; "I adore Him. But you can't expect me to change my nature."

He went on to explain that his nature was proud, rebellious, and acquisitive. "I am a collector," he said, and looked around him proudly. Just the same, he realized that Hell was becoming crowded beyond its capacity; and gazing downward to where ever fresh multitudes were entering through the gates, he remarked with a sigh:

"Really, I am up to my . . ."

At that moment, catching sight of the delicious shades of Francesca da Rimini and Madame de Pompadour strolling nearby, he stopped himself in mid-sentence, made a leg, and continued in altered tones:

"We have too many souls here."

Asmodeus, who was standing beside him, exclaimed at this evidence of refinement. But Lucifer continued:

"As a matter of fact, I have thought for a long time that we are going about this the wrong way. A soul is such an immaterial thing, it is unworldly, it does nothing while on earth, and can be said to exist only here or in Heaven. And it is so easily caught, besides: one has only to be observant, and quick, and to get there before the priest. While on the other hand, the human heart . . . ah, my friends, that is a horse of another color, that is what gets things done. The heart beats in the world, and creates empires and dynasties; it is the greatest architect of history. Where else will you find the loftiest dreams combined with the most childish anxieties? And what else gives birth to charity, to orphanages and foundations, and to crimes of every kind, as well as the most beautiful symphonies and love stories?"

He gazed around him with a gloomy expression. "Who has won the most hearts?" he asked. "Ourselves—or You-Know-Who? We have a thousand souls to His one; but on earth as in Heaven, He gets the love."

Lilith, who was in the group surrounding him, gave a voluptuous sigh. "Love," she said. And she gazed hopefully at a famous motion-picture star, who returned her gaze in a confused manner. His arm was linked with that of Alcibiades, the son of Clineas, the Athenian.

The great Archangel strode up and down, pondering. "It is much easier to hate than to love," he said at last. "To hate is to exclude, to love is to accept, to draw in . . . which calls for a different set of muscles. To say No is to finish something; to say Yes is to begin it. I wish I had hearts to love me, on earth."

At this, one of the surrounding shades stepped eagerly forward. He wore his hair in a curving bang over his forehead, and had a small mustache directly beneath his nose. Holding out his arm in a stiff salute, he exclaimed,

"*Sieg Heil!*"

"*Heil,*" said Lucifer.

"My Leader," cried the shade. "Let us not bother our heads about love, which is only for cowards and Jews! We are all heroes here. Hate! That is the thing! Let us have our hearts filled with hate, as we had at home!"

So saying, he stepped back, with a satisfied air. "Thank you, Adolf," said Lucifer.

"It is nothing."

"No," admitted Lucifer sadly, "it is nothing."

It was agreed that something must be done, that a new evangel should be sent to earth to buy men's hearts rather than their souls. But there was no agreement as to how this mission should be organized, or who was to head it; for every lost soul was convinced, just as he had been on earth, that he was right and everybody else was wrong. There were outcries, and some hair-pulling; and several fist fights developed, particularly among those whose lives had been devoted to politics, or musical criticism.

In the end—as he had expected—Lucifer was obliged to make up his own mind. Calling to his side the Archdemon Samael of Hod, he addressed him in the elevated style that he reserved for such occasions.

"We have been together a long time, dear friend," he said; "as long as I can remember. For you were one of the original band who shared with me those glorious days among the Cherubs and with my brothers, the Seraphim, before disaster overtook us. In fact, you are considered in the *Bahir,* or *Yerushalmi* of the Kabalah, to have been the one who accosted Eve, riding upon a serpent

or a camel, depending upon the vowel points. Ah
me! Those regions of light and joy! I know that
you, too, think of them with regret."

Samael, who had heard Lucifer speak in this
vein before, looked anxiously at his master. What
is coming now? he thought.

The fallen Seraph continued:

"Now hear this. I have chosen you, Samael of
Hod, to undertake a great—and possibly last—mission to the world, since it is possible that man will
blow himself up very shortly, thereby wiping himself off the face of the earth. The thought of being
obliged to court the cockroaches—who may be all
that is left—depresses me. I want to gather a few
men's hearts, as many as possible, while there is
still time."

"Oh," said Samael, "that's it.

"Women too?"

"Certainly," said Lucifer, somewhat surprised.
"Women too. Why not?"

The corners of Samael's mouth drew down.

"They have always been troublemakers," he declared. "My head still aches from being stepped on in the Garden; I can still hear those awful words: 'It shall bruise thy head and thou shalt bruise his heel.'"

"Nevertheless," said Lucifer. He laid a kindly arm around Samael's shoulder. "As far as headaches go," he said, "don't forget that I fell a long ways, too."

"Who could forget it?" asked Samael glumly.

Lucifer then told him that he had just received an offer from the United States of America. "It comes from a Mr. Alfred Sneeden," he said, "a resident of the town of Parish, in the county of the same name. I believe that Parish, however, is not the county seat. Mr. Sneeden desires youth, and a certain young lady named Gladys Milhouser. Remember the name. He offers the usual. . . . I want you to arrange to take his heart instead."

The demon gave Lucifer a piteous look. "Do I have to?" he asked.

Lucifer inclined his head.

"If only it weren't the United States," said Samael with a sigh. "It is up to its . . ."

"Careful," said Lucifer. "There are ladies present."

"It is full of evangelists," said Samael weakly.

"There is a difference," said Lucifer. "We don't ask for contributions."

Still with his arm around Samael's shoulder, and spreading his dark, enormous wings, Lucifer flew to a side door, which he opened with an iron key. A blast of icy cold struck Samael in the face. Turning, he looked back for a moment at the warm firelight, the billowing clouds stained by the glow of sulphurous fires, the bustle and clatter of Hell. "Geronimo!" he cried; and taking a deep breath, stepped out into space.

"Good luck," said Lucifer. "Keep us posted."

CHAPTER 4

Two days later, Dr. Samuel Hod opened an office
in Parish. According to the handbills distributed
to the local merchants, and an advertisement in
the county newspaper, Dr. Hod specialized in
"vascular diseases, internal medicine, disorders of
the heart, hardening of the arteries and other
symptoms of age, with special attention to the
rejuvenating process as prescribed by such emi-
nent Doctors as Fludd, Starkey, Glauber, Boyle,

Dammy, Kunst, Lenzoni, J. Scheible, Everard, Flussus, and Bernard of Treves. With use of the Thermistone. Hours, 10 A.M. to 12; 3 P.M. to 5. Consultation free."

Old Dr. Fleming, who had taken care of the people of Parish for more than twenty years, was indignant, and assured his wife that only a charlatan would advertise himself like that. But after a visit to Dr. Hod's office, he had to admit that the new doctor appeared to be well educated in medicine. "He's got diplomas from Göttingen, Harvard, and Heidelberg on his walls," he said. "That is, if they're real."

"Did you see the Thermistone," asked Mrs. Fleming, "or whatever it's called?"

Dr. Fleming shook his head. "No," he said, "I didn't. He must have had it in another room. It's probably some sort of radiant-heat machine . . . maybe for the treatment of rheumatism. I didn't ask, and he didn't offer."

"Well," said Mrs. Fleming, "I think it's a shame,

his coming here like this and trying to take your practice away from you after all these years."

"Oh," said Dr. Fleming, "I don't think he'll do that." He paused for a moment, and then added slowly:

"I don't even think he wants to."

Mrs. Fleming gave an audible sniff. "Humph," she said. If he didn't want her husband's practice, what had he come for? "Were there many patients in his waiting room?" she asked.

"There weren't any," said Dr. Fleming. "I had a feeling that he didn't care."

He stood scratching his chin in a puzzled way. "The thing I can't figure out," he said at last, "is what brought him here."

"That's what I mean," she said; "what indeed?

"Is he young, or old?"

Dr. Fleming thought for a moment. "He could be either," he declared. "The veins on his hands don't show, but his ears are leathery."

Mrs. Fleming gave another sniff. "That doesn't

tell me very much," she complained. "Would you say he was nice-looking?"

Dr. Fleming made an uncertain gesture with his elbows. "I'd say he was noticeable," he said.

Dr. Hod had no difficulty in establishing himself in Parish, for in addition to his diplomas, his bank references were impeccable.

Besides, as Dr. Fleming had observed, he was a noticeable figure in a town which was not used to strangers. Mr. Venner, of Venner's Funeral Parlors, thought him a very distinguished-looking man. "I wouldn't want to guess his age," he remarked, "but I'd say if he's over fifty he's remarkably well preserved."

On the other hand, Miss Olney, who ran the dress shop, found him a little frightening. "He has this way," she said, "like he could see right through you." And clutching her cardigan more closely around her, she retired behind a stack of dresses. She wished to put as much material as possible between herself and the new doctor.

It didn't take Samael very long to look over the situation and to lay his plans. It would have been a simple matter to seek out Alfred Sneeden, go up to him, and remark: "You called me, and here I am." But Samael had had experience in these matters, and he knew only too well what would happen: Sneeden would jump right out of his skin, and deny everything.

Therefore, the thing to do was to get him into the office, and win his confidence. But for that, he needed the right bait.

Humming a tune from Boito's *Mephistopheles,* he set off for the drugstore, where he hoped to find Gladys Milhouser.

As he had expected, he discovered her already seated at the soda fountain with several of her friends. Samael sat down at the other end of the long counter, next to the magazines, and stared at her.

Little by little, under his gaze which rested on the back of her neck, the girl's assurance began to desert her, her vivacity seemed to drain out of her, her smiles grew fewer, her conversation dried up, and she lapsed into silence. And when at last, unwillingly, she turned her head and faced him, she gave a gasp, closed her eyes, and moved by an obscure emotion, felt to make sure that the buttons on her blouse were fastened.

A moment later, unable to help herself, she opened her eyes and looked at him and was unable to look away.

"What's the matter, Glad?" asked one of her companions. "You get a bad nut or something?"

"No," said Gladys, still staring at Samael. "Why?"

"It sounded like you went 'Oh,' or something," said her friend.

"Excuse me," said Gladys; "I got to go."

Slowly, in a sort of daze, but with immense dignity, she got up and went to the ladies' room. When she came back, she had put fresh lipstick on her mouth, which was now, more than ever, shaped like a Cupid's bow. Moving along the length of the counter to where Samael was sitting, she let herself down beside him.

"Hi," she said.

When he smiled back at her, she felt a warmth such as she had never felt before; it seemed not so much to warm her skin as to reach downward to her bones. He's cool, she murmured to herself. He's real cool.

And with a mysterious expression, she remarked:

"Haven't I seen a picture of you somewheres?"

Samael disclaimed being a celebrity. "However," he assured her, "you might have seen my advertisement; I have just started a medical practice here."

"Oh," she breathed, opening her eyes to their widest; "you're the new doctor."

He had long ago decided not to waste any time. "Yes, I am," he said. "And I believe that you can help me."

He explained to her that he needed a receptionist for his office. "I've only just opened, you see," he said, "and I don't know anyone.

"It needn't be for very long," he added; "merely for the summer. Perhaps you have a friend . . . ?"

Her senses still swam a little, and she wasn't too sure what he meant. "Well, I don't know," she said; "I really don't."

"The hours are easy," he went on persuasively: "from ten to twelve, and from three to five. Three hours for lunch; and of course a morning and afternoon coffee break."

"I see," she said, and swayed in his direction.

"The pay is good," said Samael, "and—for the right girl—there might even be a bonus at the end of the summer."

And gazing deeply into her eyes, he murmured: "How about it?"

Gladys gazed back at him. She saw him in a fog, but she had not lost her vocabulary. He's neat, she thought. Neato.

"What did you say?" she breathed, through half-parted lips as soft as flowers.

"I said: how about it?"

For some reason he felt himself growing less assured. She was not at all like the young ladies he was accustomed to deal with. For one thing, she didn't seem to be in the least afraid of him. In fact, in a way, she almost seemed to be enjoying herself.

He continued a little nervously:

"Would you . . . yourself . . . consider it . . .?"

But he realized that for the moment, at least, he had lost the offensive. He felt that in Miss Milhouser he had encountered something for which he had not been prepared, and that a retreat was in order. Rising gracefully to his feet before she could answer, he threw some silver coins onto the counter. "Think it over," he said. "I'll be in my office all day."

On his way back, he passed Miss Olney's dress shop, and seeing the proprietress staring out at him, he tipped his hat to her in an Old World gesture. Miss Olney put her hands to her face, and retired once more behind the rack of dresses,

where she felt safe. The thought that she might
have been looked through again, caused her the
utmost embarrassment.

Meanwhile, in their usual places in front of the
counter with its gleaming faucets and spigots, and
its round trays of cakes and pies under glass,
Gladys and her friends were talking it over. "I'd
never have the nerve," said Sally Ewart; "going up
to a stranger like that.

"Imagine!"

Gladys tossed her head and swung her hair to
and fro. She was excited, and her eyes seemed to
be slightly crossed. "He's not a stranger, exactly,"
she said. "He's the new doctor."

"Sure," said Henry Muggins; "he's the one just
opened an office in town here. They say he's a
quack."

Gladys' eyes uncrossed themselves in a hurry.
"Who says so?" she demanded.

"Oh . . . people," said Henry vaguely. "You
know . . . everybody."

She drew herself erect, cold as a schoolmarm in

her chair. "I think you'd better not repeat things like that," she said, "that you could regret. I mean, passing remarks about what you don't know anything about. Okay?

"Because," she added, having only that moment made up her mind, "I'm going to work for him this summer."

Sally Ewart let out a squeal, and embraced her; but Henry, who had been going steady with Sally for the past two years and had been thinking of making a change-over to Gladys, stared at her in dismay. All of a sudden, it appeared, girls were grown up; they became people, and went to work in an office. It wasn't fair.

"Big deal," said Henry. "Big deal!"

CHAPTER 5

It wasn't long before Alfred was in receipt of the two pieces of information which were so soon to change his life, though not in the way he expected. He had already received one of Samael's announcements to the local merchants; and the further news that Gladys Milhouser was going to work for the new doctor caused him to seek an appointment as soon as possible.

Gladys' father, Leo Milhouser, had no objection

to his daughter keeping herself busy over the summer. There wasn't much for a girl to do once school was out, except to amuse herself; and every parent knew what that could lead to. A job like that of a receptionist in a doctor's office seemed to him a very comfortable solution to the problems of a young woman with too much time on her hands and a prize-winning figure.

Besides—work never hurt anybody. He himself belonged to the Kiwanis, the Lions, and the Junior Chamber of Commerce, and he believed in the sanctity of American institutions, among which, high on the list, stood the professions of law and medicine. "Just so long as he joins Rotary," he declared, "that's good enough for me."

Mrs. Milhouser, in whose mind life was a series of narrow escapes, knew better than to disagree with him. Not that she herself had ever been in danger, but one never knew. "Always keep the door open," she said to her daughter, "and the minute he tries to give you a pill, come home at once." It was better to be quick than sorry, and a mother owed her child at least that much preparation for life.

"Oh, Mother!" said Gladys. "Really!" She thought her mother was funny; she thought all older people were funny. She was quite sure that she could take care of herself, if she wanted to.

And Samael gave her no reason to think otherwise. The office was quiet, the work was easy, the doctor was, if anything, too polite and impersonal. She had expected something a little more exciting, after that first meeting in the drugstore. Still, the summer was young.

Nor did the appearance of Alfred Sneeden in the waiting room cause her any concern. She supposed he was simply a patient, and that his flushed face and trembling hands were symptoms of a disease. "You can go right in," she said; "the doctor will see you."

It was the most she had ever said to him, and he intended to remember it forever.

Dr. Hod remained seated as Alfred was shown in, thinking that it would give his visitor more confidence—that if he rose and shook him by the hand, he might appear to be either too eager or too little the *magister medicus*. For the same reason, while he took down Alfred's history in a large, hasty scrawl on a loose piece of paper within a yellow manila folder, he tried to keep his expression firm, knowledgeable, and alert, but also understanding and tender. He was successful, and the effect was what he wanted. "The thing is," said Alfred confidentially, "I'm feeling sort of run-down. If you know what I mean." And he gave Samael a timid wink.

"Rheumatic, perhaps?" asked Samael, studying his notes. "A touch of anemia? Calcium deposits?"

"No," said Alfred, taken aback. "That is . . . no. No, sir."

He paused a moment, studying the doctor with wary eyes. "I read what you said in your advertisement about getting old," he said slowly, "and about being able to rejuvenate . . ."

"Ah yes," said Samael heartily. "Symptoms of age. Prostatitis. . . . Do you have pain when passing water?"

Alfred was shocked. "No," he said; "no, sir. There's no pain. I mean, there's nothing the matter with me."

He took a deep breath. "I thought maybe you could make me young again," he said. "That's all."

The demon pursed his lips thoughtfully and brought the tips of his fingers together. "Why not?" he replied.

"Of course," he added, "you realize that what you ask is rather expensive. I mean to say—one doesn't expect that kind of treatment for nothing—does one?"

And he smiled warmly at Alfred. "I can do it, certainly," he declared. "But are you prepared to pay for it?"

Alfred hesitated; and his heart sank. It was true, then—but perhaps it would be too expensive.

"How much would it be?" he asked. "I haven't too much cash."

Samael held up his hand in gentle reproof. "It's not a question of money," he said.

He rose, and coming around the desk, grasped Alfred firmly by the hand. "I can't tell you how glad I am that you came to me," he said, "because I am not here to make money, but to help."

He continued in an open and friendly way: "I must tell you that I work for a great Foundation, among whose aims and goals is the study and understanding—the use, one might almost say—of man. In other words, how to use man's virtues and powers to the very best advantage.

"So you see, you have come to the right place."

As he spoke, he gazed persuasively into Alfred's eyes, which began to swim. But at the same time they were filled with strange visions of delight, while in his ears he heard the most ravishing and comforting sounds.

"Besides," the doctor was saying, "think of the advantages of being young. To wake every day in health, to be filled with joy and optimism, to have your heart's desire . . . the warm arms and tender breasts of a young woman . . .

"No, my friend, there are things of far greater value than money in the world. The gift of self, for instance; or even the grant of some small part of one's self . . .

"It is this which is of interest to my profession."

Reaching behind him, he took from his desk a printed form. "I have here a contract," he said; "or, if you prefer, we can call it a conditional grant. In it, you agree to deliver to us your heart, in good condition, warm and loving, at such and such a time, without escheat or hindrance, in fee simple, to have and hold . . . and so forth and so forth. It is really quite easy. All you have to do is sign it, and we can begin the treatments at once."

But Alfred had not altogether lost track of his senses. "Yes," he said, "that's all very well—but I need my heart myself, don't I? How will I breathe? I'd be dead."

Samael hastened to reassure him on this point.

"After all," he declared, "an agreement such as this is only a formality. We are in no hurry; indeed, we are quite willing to wait until you are finished with it."

"Well, now," said Alfred, "that's something else again."

He still hesitated; but he could find nothing wrong with it: when he was finished with his heart, what would he want with it? As far as he could see, it was like leaving your bones to a medical school, or your eyes to an eye-bank.

At that precise moment, as he teetered between yes and no, Gladys, having been summoned by Samael (she remembered only later that the buzzer had not yet been installed in the office), entered the room and inquired:

"Did you want me, Doctor?"

(Was it possible that she heard aright? And that Dr. Hod had actually replied: "It is this gentleman who wants you"? Surely not!)

(And was it possible that to Alfred, for one

breathless second, she appeared clothed only in a frilly cotton nightgown?)

"I'll sign," he said hoarsely, and reached for the contract.

"That is all, Miss Milhouser," said Samael pleasantly, slipping the signed contract into his pocket. "Now, Mr. Sneeden, if you'll just step this way. . . ."

From the room in which he kept his black box which he called the thermistone, came a light humming. Miss Milhouser wasn't sure what it was: it might have been an electric motor, or it could have come from Dr. Hod himself.

CHAPTER 6

"Look here," said Father Deener to his friend the postmistress, "there's something peculiar about this."

He and Mary Sebastian were having tea together in his study lined with books whose old leather bindings, soiled and often tattered, gleamed like ancient treasures in the lamplight. Father Deener was proud of his library, which he had accumulated over the years, and in which he numbered the works of Augustine, Origen, Aristotle, Philo, and Cardinal Newman, as well as Everard's translation of *The Divine Pymander,* and *The Mysterium Magnum* of Bernard of Treves.

And holding out to Miss Sebastian his copy of the *Magnum,* which had been published in 1510, he exclaimed:

"Can there be two Bernard of Treves, separated by more than four hundred years?"

Miss Sebastian agreed that it seemed unlikely.

"What is more," continued the priest in troubled tones, "some of these other names have a strangely familiar sound."

And going to the shelf, he drew down the first volume of Shrafft's *History of Alchymy and Magic,* and opened it to the index. "It is as I thought," he murmured; "they are all mentioned here: Fludd, Glauber, Boyle, Dammy . . .

"Good heavens!

"I think it is time I went to see this Dr. Hod myself."

"Surely, Father," said Mary, "you don't expect him to be four hundred years old?"

Father Deener crossed himself. "I only hope he isn't older still," he said bleakly.

He found the doctor in his office, his hands behind his back, staring moodily out of the window. Father Deener was surprised to find Gladys Milhouser seated on the secretary's chair, drenched in tears. The young girl's face was all the more charming for the water which brimmed out of her eyes and ran down her cheeks. "If I am intruding in any way," said the priest apologetically, "I can come back later."

Samael assured him that he was not intruding, and dismissing Miss Milhouser, who made a slight genuflection to Father Deener as she left, the demon remarked:

"She cannot even spell *microposopus!*"

"Neither can I," said Father Deener forthrightly,

"but I can spell well enough to read my history, and I know that one of your references lived in A.D. 1638, and another in 1739."

Samael shrugged his shoulders. "The famous essay by Harvey on the circulation of the blood," he remarked, "was published in 1628. And Theophrastus Bombast, born in 1493, and known to you as Paracelsus, introduced the medical profession to psychosomatic disorders, and also to a primitive form of post-inoculation. I refer, of course, to the *mumia*, although I am obliged to admit that he rather let his imagination run away with him. So my references are from the past, but what is time, Father? To the Eternal, it does not exist."

"Amen," said Father Deener mechanically.

Turning again to the window, Samael gestured at the crowds walking to and fro on the street below. "Look there," he exclaimed: "regard your townspeople; half of them cannot spell 'Mississippi.' And many of them cannot even read the works of men who strove all their lives to give them courage and love."

He smiled a little wryly. "I suppose I ought not to care," he admitted; "but I cannot help it."

He continued: "The truth is, I have such pity for the human race! To have tried so hard, to have evolved so far—and not to have evolved any further! To have indulged in the loftiest dreams, to have enjoyed the most divine hopes—to have discovered imagination, and invented religion—and to die just the same, the day after tomorrow. . . .

"So much, for so little!"

"Do you then," cried Father Deener, "believe that this earthly life is all there is? That there is no hereafter, and that the universe is empty?"

"Certainly not," exclaimed Samael at once. "I know better than that. And so do you, Father. I am thinking only of the human condition. To have struggled so long and with such infinite pains to learn to speak—which is in itself an astounding display of virtuosity—to have invented the wheel, learned the use of fire, of poisons, and of nutritional grains, to have thought up the use of symbols, first to express ideas, and later the alphabet (which is another act of surprising ingenuity)— to have learned, through what a long and agonizing process, to love . . . to have, in short, invented mankind, and yet to be unable to save it. . . ."

"You have a great deal of sympathy for the human race," said Father Deener in surprise.

"Indeed," replied Samael, "I am full of it. My first prescription was given solely out of compassion: I saw a man and a woman living together in a state of ignorance, and attempted to stimulate their imagination with a massive dose of *pyrus malus*. The results exceeded all expectations."

And without meaning to, he rubbed the top of his head where Eve had stepped on it with her heel. The gesture was noticed but misunderstood by Father Deener, who thought it merely a nervous mannerism; nevertheless, he stepped back and repeated in a firm voice:

"Get thee behind me, Satan!"

Samael gazed at the priest in astonishment; it had been a long time since he had last heard those words. They had no effect on him, but out of courtesy he went and stood behind Father Deener; however, he made it appear as though he had some business there. After a while he observed gently:

"We are not in the Middle Ages now, Father. I am a member of the County Medical Association."

Shaken and mystified, Father Deener stopped in at the post office on his way home. "Something is going on," he informed Miss Sebastian, "but I don't know what. Ought I inform the Bishop? Or the Monsignor? There was a definite odor of brimstone in the doctor's office, but of course it might have come from Venner's Funeral Parlors down the street."

Miss Sebastian was inclined to agree with Father Deener that there was something strange about the new doctor. "It's funny," she observed, "but in all the time he's been here, he hasn't had a single letter. It makes you wonder." But she advised against doing anything rash. "You can never be sure, these days," she said. "People turn out to be almost anything. For all you know, he may belong to the F.B.I., or the Birch Society."

Father Deener sighed. "It is strange, is it not," he said, "that the man who is leading this nation to its greatest attack of biliousness should be a candy manufacturer!"

Miss Sebastian pursed her lips, and shook her head disapprovingly. "I don't think you ought to mix yourself up in politics, Father," she declared.

"You are right, Mary," said Father Deener: "there is truth everywhere. A priest cannot afford to take sides, except between good and evil."

And he stepped back from the window to allow Miss Olney to place upon the counter a package she wished sent by special handling to a customer in a neighboring town. "That will be forty cents," said Miss Sebastian. "How have you been feeling?"

"Poorly," said Miss Olney, fishing in her purse for the change. "I don't sleep very well, either."

And turning to Father Deener, she added with an air of alarm:

"There are owls where I live."

"Owls also are God's creatures," remarked Father Deener gently.

Miss Olney drew a deep breath. "One doesn't know who to trust," she said as she turned away from the window.

Father Deener stamped angrily out of the post office. "There you have it," he said to himself; "nobody trusts anybody any more."

And hurriedly entering his church, he made his way to the chapel and knelt before the Virgin, whose calm and open countenance gazed down at him without altering its expression. "Lady," he said, "Lady and Mother, you trusted the Angel Gabriel when he came to announce the birth of a Son. By every natural law it was impossible, but you accepted the impossible. Help me to remember that I do not really know my right hand from my left, since in eternity the right and the left may be interchangeable.

"Do not let the Powers of Darkness deprive me of my ignorance which has been so full of innocence and joy. Do not let me be like Thomas, who doubted everything unless he could put his finger in it, but let me rather take after Peter, who believed that he could walk upon the water, until he fell in."

Crossing the chancel of the little church, he bowed himself before the altar. "Thy will, Lord," he said humbly. "If Satan is here among us, I am sure You know it; so there is no reason for me to feel worried."

He returned home, where his cook who came to work for a few hours each day had left a pot of stew simmering for him on the stove. "After all," he said, fishing a carrot, an onion, and a bone full of succulent marrow out of the pot, "it is a great comfort to have something to believe in; and where one thing is as possible as another, a person would be foolish not to believe in the power and glory of God, the intercession of saints, and the coming and going of angels."

At that moment an owl hooted in the garden outside, where dusk had already fallen, and Father Deener made haste to cross himself. "Unfortunately," he murmured, "what is true for one is equally true for another; and if the Holy Virgin can appear on earth to mortal eyes, as she has repeatedly done in France and Italy, why not those demons who used to appear to the hermits of the Thebaid in the form of maidens with melting looks and scaly bodies? Or, for that matter, in the form of a doctor promising eternal youth . . . ?"

He snapped his fingers, and sat bolt upright. "That's what he meant by Marguerite!" he exclaimed. "Her name wasn't Sneeden at all."

CHAPTER 7

Thomas McHenry, returning with his son from a business trip to the capital, brought with him a swan for the pool in the garden. It was white, with a black beak, a long, slender neck, and red eyes, and it was inflatable, being made of vinyl. The effect, seen through the trees and bushes which screened the pool, was lifelike and charming. Moved by the currents of air, the white swan floated slowly over the surface of the pool, or remained motionless and serene upon the blue waters.

Mr. McHenry found his wife, as he had expected, in poor health; she was sober, but feeling the effects. It was the garden which appeared to have suffered the most; the flower beds were disturbed as though someone had been digging in them with a trowel, and the roots of several rose bushes were exposed.

"It was Father Deener told me to," said Mrs. McHenry tearfully; "but somehow or other it got away from me."

"No matter, my dear," said Mr. McHenry gently; "we'll soon have it to rights again." He loved his wife, who was a source of endless unhappiness to him, sleeplessness, and the feeling that without her, life would be empty.

When she first saw the swan floating in the pool, she was surprised and delighted. "The way it looks," she said, "you'd think it was real." She ex-

plained that as a child she had been given a tiny
duckling painted green for Easter. "It was too
young to lay an egg," she said. "It was very small,
and it died."

Most of the time she felt that her life was a
failure. The love between a mother and her son,
about which she had read, had somehow missed
her; and she blamed her husband for displacing
her, for taking her son's love away from her. But
the truth was, she was frightened of children, who
were so defenseless and so terrible; and faced
with a decision of authority, she would run away,
and go into her room and lock the door. Then she
would begin to drink, and after a while she would
begin to feel good again, and nothing mattered;
and her husband and her son were gone off on a
fishing trip.

When she was drinking, the world was like the
inside of a colored ball, and everything was round
and bright and possible. There was no such thing
as time, or space, from-now-to-then or from-here-

to-there, it all dissolved and ran together into a
sort of hum. In the hum there were sudden sounds
. . . moments, which might be long or short, a
minute or an hour, and usually merry; it was impossible to time them, to know how long they
lasted, because they came up like lighted lamps
out of blankness, and were swallowed up in blankness again. She was not afraid of children, then;
she was not afraid of anything, even at night.
There was no emptiness around her, everything
was crowded with herself.

And it was delicious, mostly, interrupted by
moments of grief which in their own way were delicious too, being so free-flowing and peaceful; it
was like having joy without fear, and sorrow without pain. It was a time to attack rosebushes without anxiety.

But afterwards, she was like a sodden biscuit.

"Why do you put up with me?" she sometimes
asked her husband; to which he invariably replied:

"Because I love you."

It failed to convince her, or even to comfort her; she was too far gone in guilt to be able to see herself as lovable. "I wish I were dead," she declared, like a child, not meaning it; and like a child, accepting whatever he gave her, in matter or spirit. After all, she told herself sooner or later, it was his fault, not hers; he was the one to blame.

"It's when he goes off on those long trips," she told herself. "It's the emptiness."

Besides, when she was sober she was afraid at night, for night was full of dangers. She still thought sometimes—a holdover from childhood— that in the darkness tigers could come. And every day the newspapers were full of horrible stories about people being robbed and murdered.

She didn't remember when the drinking had all started. Had Tom gone off on a trip once, and left her alone with her terrors? Could it have been when she was carrying Tom Junior? Not that it mattered any more, it was too late now, anyway.

She took comfort from the swan. Seeing it floating across the water, watching from her windows
as it drifted quietly along behind the screen of
bushes which lined the pool, she felt almost as
though it was a living presence there in the garden, a companion, peaceful, unhurried, wise, and
made of vinyl. It wouldn't be going anywhere.

Dr. Fleming, passing the house on his way to
the drugstore to have some prescriptions made up,
also caught a glimpse of the swan and thought for
a startled moment that some wild bird had landed
in the McHenry pool, possibly a migrating goose or
a pelican. "I didn't get a good look at it," he explained to the pharmacist, Mr. Oates, "but it's that
natural."

He shook his head admiringly. "They certainly
do things these days," he said.

Mr. Oates agreed with him that they lived in
interesting times. "There's all these new drugs,
too," he remarked. "A fellow has to keep on his
toes to know what half of them are."

Searching around on the counter, he picked

up a prescription and showed it to Dr. Fleming. "Here's something that new doctor, Hod's his name, left with me this morning. Damned if I know what he's talking about."

Dr. Fleming glanced at the prescription, which called for 12 oz. of Red Lion, 10 oz. of White Eagle, ½ lb. pure carbonate of potash, 1 bushel melissa leaves, and 1 qt. of absolute alcohol. "Never saw anything like it," said Mr. Oates.

Dr. Fleming put the prescription back on the counter. "Neither did I," he said.

"This Red Lion," ventured Mr. Oates. "You think maybe it's some kind of likker?"

"Sounds like it to me," Dr. Fleming replied cheerfully. He pulled his own prescriptions out of his coat pocket and handed them to the pharmacist. "Make this one up for Delia McHenry," he said; "it's to quiet her down. And send the rest over to my office.

"You get hold of any absolute alcohol," he said with a wink, "you let me know."

As he was leaving, he passed Father Deener,

who was entering the drugstore to buy a bottle of aspirin. "How are you, Father," he asked, stopping a moment to shake the priest's hand. And dropping his voice an octave or two, he added:

"I hear that you paid a call recently on Delia McHenry."

"Ah yes," said Father Deener with a sigh; "the poor woman; it did no good, I fear. I'm afraid that I lacked the necessary moral force."

He hesitated a moment. "Tell me, Doctor," he said presently, "do you think that two aspirins in a glass of hot milk might help to induce sleep?"

"You might try a little whiskey with it," said Dr. Fleming carelessly. His gaze fell once more on Dr. Hod's prescription, lying face up on the counter. "One half ounce of good old Red Lion," he said. "Before retiring."

And with a friendly wave of his hand, he went out of the door. "Did he say Red Lion?" asked Father Deener. "That's odd."

"I guess he was joking," said Mr. Oates. He

picked up the prescription and held it out to him. "Whatever it is," he said, "old Doc couldn't make any more out of it than me."

Father Deener studied the small rectangular piece of paper, his lips pursed and a thoughtful look in his eyes. "Does it mean anything to you, Father?" asked Mr. Oates curiously.

"I think so," said Father Deener. "I seem to have seen this somewhere before . . ."

Taking his bottle of aspirin, he went home to his study, where he took from the shelf an ancient volume bound in leather. Blowing the dust away, and opening it to the section on alchemy, he turned the pages until he came to what he was looking for. He read swiftly, occasionally nodding his head; at last he looked up with a strange expression.

"I was right," he said softly. "It is the Primum Ens."

CHAPTER 8

Alfred Sneeden, studying himself in the mirror, decided that he did indeed look younger, and to his own eyes at least better-looking. He was parting his hair differently now, and using one of those hair oils advertised on television, the one where the young fellow was always whistling at some girl and she was kissing and nuzzling him and running her fingers through his hair. It didn't take much for a man to get a girl; just being young and using hair oil.

He felt grateful to Dr. Hod for starting his treatments so promptly. But as far as the contract was concerned, he hardly gave it a thought. He was healthy, he felt good, and he breathed regularly; now and then he found himself a little more lighthearted than usual, but it was an agreeable sensation, his normal spirits being so low.

In fact, there was only one thing that troubled him: Gladys, for whose sake he was doing all this, didn't seem to notice the change in him. He saw her every day now; but their relationship—she sitting businesslike and properly dressed behind her desk, and he making some remark about the weather—didn't seem to be improving; she wasn't growing any warmer. He was making no progress, that was the truth: he wasn't getting anywhere.

And trying to find some reason for his failure, he complained to Dr. Hod: "There's no use my being younger if it isn't going to get me any-where."

Samael remembered that Lucifer had told him that Alfred expected to be given Miss Gladys Milhouser, and he understood that he would have to do something about it.

"Leave it to me," he said with an air of confi-dence he was far from feeling. Thereafter he set himself up to study the situation, which he real-ized presented some problems beyond his experi-ence.

The classic thing to do, he told himself, would be to send her a large bouquet of flowers, with Alfred's card attached; and perhaps a bracelet or some other trinket. But he rejected this approach as being too old-fashioned. In the world today, he reflected, the art of seduction, which once moved at the gentle pace of a waltz or a horse-and-carriage, now takes off like a rocket. And a woman, who in the past had to be peeled as carefully as an onion—first from her wrap, then from her jacket, her blouse, waist, camisole, chemise, corset-cover, corset, and underthings (how dainty, ruffled, beribboned, and smelling of lavender and other delicious odors!)—is today like an apple, demanding to be picked and eaten, peel and all.

Therefore, the sensible approach to the modern young woman must be a direct one.

And summoning Miss Milhouser into his office, he began to advertise the virtues of his client. "He is no schoolboy," he exclaimed. "He is a man of the world, devoted to the most exciting of the sciences, the use of electricity."

"You mean he fixes radios," said Gladys.

"From there," said Samael, "it is only a step to the stars."

He was surprised at the way Miss Milhouser was looking at him. "Yes," he repeated obstinately, "the stars. With the proper help, there is no limit to what a man can attain. I am speaking, of course, of female help. That is to say, the love of a woman . . ."

He decided not to say a good woman. But Gladys apparently didn't see any difference. "Do you really think so?" she breathed.

"Of course," replied Samael.

He continued in the same vein. "To be young," he declared, "and to be growing younger every day, is in itself unusual. At the same time, it is a very good thing for a man to have had some experience, to be to some extent a man of the world."

Gladys continued to gaze at him and he noticed with alarm that her eyes were becoming slightly crossed. Using all his powers of persuasion, he strove to paint a portrait of Alfred as a prize that any young woman would think herself lucky to win.

At last she spoke; the sweet lips parted. "I wish you'd tell me something," she said: "something truly. I mean—you don't have to be polite or anything."

Samael thought that he had gained some measure of attention for his client, and felt relieved. "What can I tell you?" he asked warmly.

Gladys looked away shyly; then suddenly turning her full gaze upon him, she inquired:

"Are you married, or anything?"

The devil! he thought: she hasn't been paying attention to a word I've said!

"No," he snapped. "I'm not."

"I just wondered," she said. "Okay?"

She twisted a curling strand of hair around one finger. "It's funny," she said, "how all of a sudden the boys you've been going around with seem so young and, like you say, inexperienced; and then you meet somebody, like you say, who's experienced . . ."

Her voice trailed off and she cast her eyes down, blushed, and waited. Samael regarded her doubtfully. Was she talking about Alfred, or about somebody else? He thought that he had better find out.

"Don't you like Mr. Sneeden?" he asked; but he

had no sooner said the words than he knew the answer. She didn't like him.

"He's a square," she said.

And she added inconsequentially:

"I'm eighteen years old."

She was not; but she would be, before the summer was over. Casting one last, thoughtful glance at Samael, she got up and went back to her desk in the waiting room.

Dr. Hod went over to the window and looked out at the sky. It was as blue as summer; a few white clouds lay lightly above the low hills which guarded Parish from the sea. He was perplexed and uneasy; and the bump on his head was aching again. "This is not going to be as easy as I thought," he said. "We need a new approach."

On the street below, Henry Muggins went by in his car, an old convertible without a top. At his side sat Sally Ewart; the sun shone down on them, her head was on his shoulder, they were young and happy; and for a moment Samael felt an unaccustomed and unwelcome pang. What a short time they had, he thought; it would be over before they knew it. Life was no picnic. So little time! In which to be young, and to go about holding hands and kissing; and afterwards— what? Before they poured their worn-out bodies into the earth, along with their worries and their griefs, their pain, their avarice, lost dreams and foolish purposes, wealth, poverty, boredom, and the right to vote.

In the next room he could hear Gladys typing out a list he had given her. She too, he thought; there she sits, thinking her own thoughts, and not knowing what lies ahead of her. This is not exactly a Christmas present I am preparing for her.

If Alfred was disappointed that Gladys didn't seem to notice him, his reception at the post office made up for it, at least in part. "Why, Mr. Sneeden," said Mary Sebastian the first time she saw him, "what have you been doing to yourself?"

So somebody had noticed it, he thought. Blushing slightly, he managed to lean negligently against the counter and at the same time smooth his hair with one hand, the way the man did in the commercial. "Well," he said, "yes; I'm feeling pretty good these days."

The strange part of it—and what he didn't know—was that he looked no younger to Mary; it was only that she had a feeling that she was seeing him, really seeing him, for the first time. She didn't know why she had never noticed him before. He has a sorrowing face, she thought; he's a nice man. She wondered for a moment what his life was like, and whether he had a friend or a sweetheart. It's probably lonely, she thought, like most people's.

"You're looking pretty well yourself," he said. When he saw her glance up at him in surprise he felt pleased because he understood that he had, after all, said something unexpected. "Yes, ma'am," he said again, "you really look like you enjoyed your work."

[82]

A little warmth stained Mary's face, across which passed the ghost of a smile. "It keeps me busy," she admitted, "and I like to be busy. I imagine that you must enjoy your work, too, Mr. Sneeden; it must be very interesting."

Seeing her sitting there behind her window—seeing her, one might almost say, for the first time—he thought that she was not at all a bad-looking woman. For her age, that was; not a beauty, exactly, but nice. In a way, she represented the government of the United States, she represented the United States Post Office Department. For a moment she seemed almost as far beyond his reach as Gladys; and for that very reason he had a sudden desire to reach her, to say something to make her notice him and to smile at him again. "I guess you must get to know a lot of people," he said, "in a post office like this."

"That is quite true," she said pleasantly. "By the way, did you ever find your relative? Or was it a friend?"

And as he only stood and stared at her, she added:

"The lady you were looking for."

"A friend?" asked Alfred stupidly. Could she possibly be referring to Miss Milhouser? "Oh, yes," he said, trying to sound indifferent, "I believe so."

"I'm glad," she said.

But how could she have found out? He felt confused and alarmed; did people know about him already? Dr. Hod had better do something in a hurry, or it would be too late. Once people started talking . . .

He waited for her to make some further remark, but when it appeared that she had nothing more to say, he turned to go. "Well," he said awkwardly, "I'll be seeing you."

"Why, thank you," said Mary.

She sat and thought about him for a little while after he had gone. He wasn't a bad-looking man, she thought; it was a shame that he put that stuff on his hair, it would probably be perfectly

nice hair without it. And he certainly made a
good appearance for a man his age. A sorrowing
face, though, and a lonely one.

Anyway, he'd looked at her as though he'd actually seen her, and that was more than most people did.

CHAPTER 9

Father Deener enjoyed the evening visits of the postmistress to his garden, where they walked together under the trees in air cooled by the sea and made fragrant by his roses and by his thoughts, which were harmonious and kind. But he was afraid that he was keeping her from other things, and from more rewarding relationships. "I am a selfish old man," he said; "I take up entirely too much of your time."

Mary hastened to reassure him. "There is no one I would rather be with," she declared. "If I didn't have this house and this garden to come to, I wouldn't know what to do."

But the old priest refused to allow himself to be reassured, for he believed that he was upsetting the designs of nature. What every woman needed, and had a right to expect, was a family of her own; although whether Mary was too old for childbearing was something he was not prepared to say.

"Just the same," he insisted, "someday we are going to find a husband for you."

Mary protested, blushing, that marriage was the last thing on her mind. And she believed that she was telling the truth, and that the sadness she felt from time to time was due to such things as a cloudy day, or sympathy for the poor.

Indeed, if there was one emotion with which she was thoroughly familiar, it was sympathy. From her window in the post office she looked out at a world which often seemed to her as lonely as her own.

It was true that she had never had much attention paid to her. When she was a young girl in grade school, she had outspelled all the boys in her class, but had gained no other distinction. Later, behind the post-office window, there seemed even less reason for anyone to notice her —or so she thought. She was wrong; a woman is never more noticeable than back of a grating or behind a small window.

Sometimes she wished that she could discuss things with Father Deener; but a feeling of embarrassment held her back. What could she ask him? Could she say: "Father, tell me about love"? She was convinced that he knew no more about it than she did. What she felt was a confused concern for people. When he spoke about such things as marriage, she blushed and changed the subject.

Sometimes she prepared dinner for him, for he enjoyed a good meal when he got one. "A splendid sauce," he often said, "is no less God's gift for having been skillfully blended by the cook. In such an incomprehensible universe as this, the greatest consolation is the right to choose what to believe. I believe that the Catholic Church offers more consolation than any of its opponents, and that tarragon is a necessary ingredient in chicken."

"I saw Mr. Sneeden today," said Mary. "He was looking remarkably well. Do you remember— he asked me about some relative? He thinks he found her."

Father Deener stood stock-still and clapped his hand to his forehead with a groan. "Marguerite!" he exclaimed. "I meant to tell you."

And he explained to her that Marguerite was the name of the young woman whose wholesome beauty had caused the philosopher Faust to lose his soul. "He was an old man when he first saw her," he said, "but he became young again, and with the help of Satan seduced the poor child, who came to a sad end. So, of course, did Faust, although in Gounod's opera he is redeemed by angelic choirs and the prayers of his victim."

He remained silent a moment, sunk in reflection. "It is a medieval tale," he said at last, "and Gounod took some liberties with it. So, for that matter, did Goethe, whose approach was more philosophic. Nevertheless, there actually was a Johann Faust, mentioned both by the Abbot of Spanheim and by Melancthon, the story of whose life was first published in Frankfurt in 1587, and who is supposed to have signed a pact with the Devil."

Miss Sebastian smiled; but seeing that her friend was very much in earnest, she stopped smiling and became serious. "We are not living in medieval times, Father," she said gently.

"Who knows?" replied Father Deener solemnly. "Leonardo da Vinci, man of the Renaissance, considered himself modern, and with reason. Four hundred years from now we may seem as medieval to our descendants as St. Francis."

He continued: "We are a small community here in Parish, tucked away among the hills. It is always in such out-of-the-way places that miracles and other strange things occur. Who knows? Perhaps your friend has made a pact with the Devil and has suddenly become young again."

"He is not my friend," said Mary, reddening. But the solemnity of Father Deener's voice impressed her despite herself. The evening with its chillier air had drawn its shadows around them, and a dog barked far away in the hills. She looked around her a little fearfully. It was all very well for Father Deener to be joyful in ignorance; but eternity—a mystery in which anything could happen—gave her a fright. She had taken God for granted all her life; if she had seen an angel, she would have been gratified, and given thanks; she would have been startled, but not incredulous. So why not the Devil? One was as likely as the other, if she stopped to think about it. Particularly at night.

"Well," she said in a small voice, "supposing—?"

"Supposing?" echoed Father Deener testily. "Everything points to it: an unknown doctor who promises to rejuvenate the aged by means of a thermistone—whatever that may be—and whose references are from alchemists dead these hundreds of years; an aging man who suddenly grows younger; Marguerite; and this same doctor's statement to me personally, that time does not exist."

And pointing a finger at his companion, who trembled in the night air, he exclaimed:

"I believe the soul of Alfred Sneeden to be in danger."

Mary remained pale and apprehensive. She didn't know why she should feel so concerned over the fate of this man whom she scarcely knew, and could only suppose that it was out of compassion for all men who had so short a time on earth to make their dreams come true.

But it was not true that Mr. Sneeden was an aging man. Except insofar as everyone was growing older.

"What are we going to do?" she whispered.

Father Deener considered in silence before replying. He felt old and helpless, opposed to the powers of darkness, and realized that his wisdom was insufficient for the charge that had been laid upon him. The Lord is certainly on my side, he reflected, or that is to say I am on His; but I have to admit that except in the case of certain saints He has always shown a marked disinclination to mix in affairs of this kind. The good Paphnutius himself was allowed to go down to defeat in a particularly painful way, and He even left St. Anthony, that great and holy Cenobite, to support alone and without assistance a struggle with an army of demons which lasted all his life.

Surely, this is a case where the full might of the Church should be invoked and the issue joined at the very highest level, and not left to one poor parish priest whose only vision of the universe has been too shoreless and boundless to furnish him with the proper canonical authority.

"What are we to do, Father?" Mary asked

again. She felt strange; she felt that a disaster had occurred somewhere in the world. There is a curious thing about disaster, it is like a disease and can infect the innocent. She felt an evil in the dark around her, which seemed to threaten her own welfare no less than Alfred Sneeden's. "What are we going to do?" she repeated.

"I shall place the whole matter in the hands of the authorities," said Father Deener vigorously.

"I am going to see the Bishop."

CHAPTER 10

Seated on a promontory overlooking the sea, which foamed white and green on the rocks below, Samael communed with himself and with a couple of black ants of the *Formica pennsylvanicus* family. These little creatures, finding Samael in their path, stopped in their endless journeying from here to there and remained motionless and alarmed, aware, like Abraham, of an unseen Presence. "Ants," the demon addressed them, having like all angels the gift of tongues; and they replied: "Behold, we are here."

"I have no one else to talk to," said Samael apologetically.

And without further preamble, he launched into an account of his mission, and gave them a brief résumé of the situation. "What we did not take into account," he explained, "was the contrariness of a woman's heart. Even though Mr. Alfred Sneeden were to take on the attributes of Samson, Solomon, and Mr. Cary Grant, there still might be a reason for Miss Milhouser to prefer someone else."

"Prefer?" asked the larger of the two ants politely. "How can that be? And what does it mean to prefer someone else? Males and females alike fly into the air, and in a whirling galaxy of ardor, duty, and the odor of formica, conceive new generations. It would be very difficult to seek out anyone special at a time like that."

Samael agreed that it would be difficult to have a preference on such an occasion. "However," he said, "we are not talking about insects here."

"Why not?" asked the second ant. "Is there anything else?"

Samael looked down at the tiny creatures, and smiled sadly. "You are right," he said: "to an ant, there are only ants and other insects, or sometimes an animal or reptile which is devoured without their ever having had a good look at it. The screams of a mouse in the path of an army of ants is no more audible to them than the cries of a vegetable about to be sliced up and put in the soup. One hears what one hears, and nothing more.

"But tell me: do you indeed have no affections of any kind?"

At this the second ant hung her head in a self-conscious way. "I have a little beetle of whom I am very fond," she admitted; "and I like to make believe that it is my very own."

"Hush, Matilda!" exclaimed the larger of the two. "You know that everything belongs to the state and that we are not allowed to own anything ourselves. Our herds of aphids give milk to the entire community, which is the way it ought to be; it is only among the wasps and spiders that you find the curse of private property; as you know, a wasp will paralyze a grasshopper and drag it off to her nest where, I am assured, she uses it for purely selfish purposes. The same applies, in a somewhat different manner, to the spider; and so it is only natural that there should exist a state of endless warfare between these two examples of private ownership.

"How much better our own slogan: 'Ask not what your country can do for you, but what you can do for your country,' because if you don't already know what your country can do for you, you haven't been paying attention."

"Very well," said Samael: "you do not love anything. But do you hate anything?"

"Only other ants," they replied; to which the smaller of the two quickly added:

"We are frightened of ant lions."

"Ah," said Samael; "then, at least, you do have feelings of a sort, because you recognize terror. So you could be made to love, and to worship God who is in the heavens.

"Forgive me, Lucifer," he murmured, "but I cannot think of any other way of putting it."

The first ant waved her antennae in Samael's direction. "I would scarcely know how to answer that," she said, "for I do not know what you mean by the heavens. I wish that I could see you, for I can easily imagine you to be God yourself, and to be made of chitin and formic acid."

"I am not God," said Samael with a shudder. "And I am not armored. The acids which compose me are chemical derivations of hydrogen, ammonium, and nitrogen, in an ethereal or asomatous state."

The ant gave a deep sigh. "We live in a mysterious universe," she declared, "where things seem to happen for no known reason. Floods inundate our cities, upheavals of the earth destroy our edifices, entire communities are wiped out by some gigantic blow. I should like to ask you a simple question: why? We are good, and our intentions are the best. As we go about our labors we are aware of huge forms and vast forces in the world; they are strange and unknown and we do not understand them. Something towers over us, to unimaginable heights, like yourself; we thought that it was God, but you tell us that we are mistaken."

"It is Man," said Samael soberly.

"And are you Man?" asked the ant.

"No," said Samael.

"You are not God, either?"

"Like you," said Samael humbly, "I am only one of God's creatures."

"It is very confusing," said the ant. And addressing her companion, she exclaimed:

"Come, Matilda, let us go back to work, and not

try to solve that which is unsolvable."

"Wait!" said Samael. "I should like to talk to you a little more about love."

"As I have told you," replied the ant firmly, "I do not know what you mean. If you mean an enthusiasm for the community, or even for the entire family of *Formica pennsylvanicus*, I can understand you; but I believe that you are talking about something else. Perhaps you would explain what you mean by 'love'?"

"I do not know how to explain it," Samael admitted, "except to say that it exists in the heart, and that those who do not have it, suffer all their lives from the lack of it.

"But let me tell you a story which may help to make things clearer. There existed, in a small country, a man whose sweetheart was obliged to leave him and go to live in a foreign land. One day he received from his absent love a box full of dry and empty earth, in which nothing was growing. He took this to mean that she was not coming back

[101]

to him. As he leaned over it, he wept; and wherever a tear fell, moistening the earth, a green shoot made its appearance. Soon the entire box was one mass of gently waving grasses, among which were to be seen the bright hues of many flowers.

"Does not this story teach you something about love?"

"No," said Matilda.

Samael shook his head. "One should learn from this story that tears are beneficent," he said, "and that from sorrow and loss come many beautiful things. Tears and sorrow are also the fruits of love.

"It is better to weep from too much, than to suffer from too little."

The ants regarded each other with their antennae. "We suffer from a lack of moisture," the larger ant remarked thoughtfully. And Matilda added:

"I am very fond of sweets, and would suffer very much if I were unable to procure them."

"Moisture and sweets," said Samael; "that is perhaps not so very different from those desires which inflame men and women. Would you give your hearts to someone who could furnish you with these comforts?"

"Our hearts are not ours to give away," said the larger ant. "They belong to the state.

"But we will be glad to bring the matter to the attention of the Presidium."

So saying, the two insects moved away, not without dignity, through the grass which towered over them and bent and swayed above their heads like the trees of a forest. And Samael, gazing up at the clear, wide sky which seemed to reflect the noonday blue of the sea, said to himself with a sigh:

"It is true that earth is very beautiful, and that the daughters of men are fair, as related in Genesis. Perhaps it is love which makes them so, but I do not actually know any more about it than Matilda."

However, he consoled himself with the reflection that it wasn't his business to know about it. "I have been ordered to bring back a heart," he said; "not to write a book. Let us leave the understanding of love to the novelists, who know all about it."

At that moment, from her garden where the swan floated quietly in the pool, Delia McHenry heard to her astonishment the mad laughter of a loon.

Actually, it was Beelzebub, who had taken for the time being the form of the great white bird. He had just overheard Samael's last remark, and thought it very funny.

CHAPTER 11

That night, Miss Olney, peering fearfully out of her window, saw a large white object, shaped like a bird, flying above the roofs of Parish in the direction of the house which Dr. Hod had taken for the summer. As she had never seen a swan before, she took it to be either an unusually large goose or a portent of some kind, and retired to a closet, where she spent the rest of the night.

When Beelzebub arrived at Samael's house, he found his fellow demon seated before a comfortable fire, deep in thought. "Lucifer wants to know what's going on," he said after greetings had been exchanged, "and what is taking you so long."

Samael offered his old friend a cigar, and Beelzebub assumed his own shape the better to enjoy it. "Not that swans aren't very nice in their way," he remarked, stretching his feet luxuriously to the fire, "and splendid for catching fish or nibbling waterlilies, but for the higher enjoyments there is nothing like the architecture of a man. Nothing too much—but everything in place, as needed: the hands capable of the most delicate maneuvers, the taste buds tuned to the proper degree, the sense of smell not overwhelming as in the case of other land animals, the braincase large enough to invent the telescope, but not big enough to be destroyed by the sight of infinity . . . in short, Man. I shall be sorry to see him go. It will be a long while before the cockroaches discover tobacco."

"Does Lucifer still think it will be cockroaches?" asked Samael.

"Why, yes," said Beelzebub; "as far as I've heard. Don't you?"

Samael shrugged his shoulders. "Who knows?" he replied. "It may be the ants."

"The monolithic state," observed Beelzebub, drawing happily on his cigar, whose rich blue smoke curled around his nose, "rather than the individual. I think it is probably a matter of indifference to Lucifer. Shall you enjoy looking like an ant, do you think?"

Samael gave a start. "I hadn't thought of that," he said. "To tell you the truth, I've been accustomed to looking like a man for so long . . . with certain minor differences, of course."

Beelzebub laughed delightedly. "My dear friend," he exclaimed, "you forget all those years when you went around in the skin of a reptile; and before that, with the gills and fins of a fish. And do you remember the trilobite? What a dull time that was! It is only since the Garden that things have livened up a bit. They will be dull again, I'm sure, with either the ants or the cockroaches."

Carefully knocking off the ash from his cigar, he cocked a quizzical eye at his friend, who stirred uneasily. "But come," he said, "how are you making out with your little arrangement? Do you have the heart yet?"

"Only on paper," Samael confessed. "I cannot in decency ask for it before I deliver the goods."

"And the goods have not yet been delivered?"

"Not yet," said Samael unhappily. "We are in escrow."

"I see," said Beelzebub soberly. "Devil take it!"

"Devil take it," Samael agreed. "But how?"

Beelzebub brooded for a while, his saturnine face drawn in a frown. At last his features relaxed, and he snapped his fingers with an air of enthusiasm. "Have you given her a dream?" he asked.

Samael shook his head. "Then give her one!" Beelzebub urged. "There is nothing like a dream to open a girl's eyes."

And as he leaned back in his chair, his face took on a bemused expression. "I remember a case in the twenties," he said, "which concerned a young lady of the theater and a distinguished playwright. I should add that he was distinguished more for his wit than for his looks, and that she also was distinguished, not only for her beauty but for her virtue. He desired her, of course; but she kept evading him by jumping over sofas, for she had been a champion high-jumper in college. One night she saw him in a dream, with a very large and fleshy nose. The next day, unable to hurdle even a low coffee table, she succumbed in his arms."

So saying, Beelzebub resumed his suit of vinyl, and with one last puff of his cigar, left by the window. His last words to Samael were to press forward, and to lose no more time. "The world may blow up at any moment," he said, "and Lucifer wants his heart before it happens."

That night Gladys Milhouser had a strange dream. She was in a moonlit garden, and on every bush there was a rose. The roses all looked like Alfred Sneeden, and each had an enormous nose.

Dr. Hod, arriving in his office the next morning, found her silent and a little pale. Beelzebub was right, he thought joyfully, we have pierced her armor.

And rubbing his hands together, he approached her with a smile and in a cheerful manner. "Well, well," he exclaimed jovially, "how is the beautiful Miss Milhouser this morning?"

To his dismay, she raised a face to him streaked with tears. "Do you really think I'm beautiful?" she asked in a dying voice, devouring him with her gaze.

Taken by surprise, the demon floundered. "Why, of course!" he exclaimed. "Naturally . . . I mean to say . . ."

A moment later, gathering himself together, he managed to insinuate: "Might it not be more important what a certain Mr. Alfred Sneeden . . . for instance . . . might have to say . . . rather than myself?"

"That's what you think!" Gladys replied, and burst into tears.

Fishing for her compact, she opened the little mirror and gazed dismally at herself. "My nose is shiny," she said, and gave a small hiccup.

"You'll have to excuse me," she said, dabbing at herself with the powder puff. "I didn't sleep very well last night. I had this bad dream?"

Her voice rose slightly, as in a question. Samael heard her with a sinking heart. The dream, then, hadn't worked as expected.

"It's bad enough," she said, "to have that creep coming into the office every day and giving me those looks . . . but to have to see him as a rose? And with a nose like a . . . like a sausage?"

I shouldn't have listened to Beelzebub, thought Samael; he's much more at home in the theater than in a quiet place like this. I should have let her see Mr. Sneeden as a knight—a shining knight . . .

"So now,"Gladys was saying drearily, "when I see a rose garden, what do I do?" And again the tears fell from those eyes for whose regard Alfred Sneeden had been willing to sell his soul.

"My dear young lady," murmured Samael in dismay; "Miss Milhouser . . . Gladys . . ."

As suddenly as the floods had started, they ceased, and she turned a shyly beaming look on him. "I never heard my name said like that," she declared. "I like it better than Glad. That's what my friends call me, Glad. Only, I like the way you say it better. You know . . . like Gladys."

"Well, then," said Samael cheerfully, "suppose we dry our eyes and get to work?"

"Yes, sir," said Gladys. She rose, still with a slight hiccup, and turned toward the files. "As a matter of fact," she said, with a certain childish dignity, "I enjoy working here very much. I mean, I'm learning a great deal, and everything."

She gave Samael one last glance, warm, and young, and disturbing. "I mean, I really do enjoy it," she said.

During the morning, Samael, as Dr. Hod, treated

an old gardener who complained of a cold and a sore throat. "Stay out of drafts," Samael told him, "and when you go to sleep at night, wrap an old woolen sock around your throat, the older the better. This will act as a sort of *mumia,* and will help to draw out the distempers."

"Han't you got a pill or something?" demanded the gardener. "Dr. Fleming, he ullus give me a pill or something."

Samael wrote him out a prescription. "Here," he said; "take this to the drugstore. And next time, please go back to Dr. Fleming. I have no desire to take his practice away from him."

When the old man had gone, Samael sat down to await the arrival of his one and only patient. He wondered what sort of greeting Mr. Sneeden would get from Gladys. It will be a discouraging one, I fear, he said to himself, and shook his head in perplexity.

He was right; beyond a cool "Good morning," no words were exchanged between the young woman and the ardent and already youthful-appearing man. "How long is this going to take, Doc?" Alfred demanded, as he sat, stripped to the waist, in front of the black box. "It's been going on two weeks now, and nothing to show."

"It is a difficult operation," said Samael. "Try to be patient."

"All right," said Alfred darkly; "but it had better be soon, on account of I haven't got forever."

Samael repressed an impulse to reply, like Gladys: "That's what you think," and instead contented himself with pointing out that just as in the repairing of a television set, nothing could be done in a hurry. "You know how things are," he said; "doesn't it always take twice as long as expected?"

"We-ell," said Alfred uncomfortably.

"Think of yourself," said Samael, "as a twenty-one-inch color set, in for repair."

Alfred's face fell. "Doc," he said hoarsely, "at that rate I'll never make out at all."

That night Beelzebub visited with Samael again, and after commiserating with him over the way

the dream had turned out, came up with still another suggestion. "It is obvious that this Sneeden
fellow can't manage his own courtship," he said,
"so you'll just have to manage it for him. You know
—like Cyrano de Bergerac with Roxanne. My advice to you is this: take her out dancing. Then,
when you have her snuggled in your arms . . ."

"Please!" groaned Samael. "Haven't I troubles
enough? What, may I ask, am I supposed to do
when she is . . . as you say . . ."

Beelzebub dismissed this question with an airy
wave of his hand. "Since you are not doing this for
yourself," he remarked, "you should be able to
keep your thoughts on higher things. In any case,
whether you like it or not, it is your duty."

"All I know is the waltz," said Samael gloomily,
"and the minuet, the lancers, and the Highland
fling."

"I'll send you a friend of mine, a delicious little
basilisk, to teach you the twist," said Beelzebub
cheerfully. "Her name is Hildegarde, and she is
from the Cortex of Sathariel."

Reaching for the cigar box, he put several cigars in his pocket. "Don't look so glum, my friend," he remarked. "I'm sure you will enjoy it. And as for the waltz—forget it; be glad they don't do it any more. The waltz was purely a means of seduction. Today's dances are more in the nature of a conflict, in which, however, no one wins."

With these words, Beelzebub took his leave through the window, as before.

At about the same time, Mr. Oates, the pharmacist, was puzzling over another prescription, brought to him by an old man with a cold. "Look at this," he said to Dr. Fleming, who was in the drugstore to pick up some peppermint drops for his wife; "sulphur and molasses. I haven't seen anything like that for nigh on to forty years."

"Ah well," said Dr. Fleming philosophically, "it's a prime purifier. Old-fashioned, perhaps, but there's no harm in it."

"But with a pinch of brimstone?" asked Mr. Oates.

CHAPTER 12

Samael took Gladys dancing at Scotti's Tavern, which stood among the pines looking out to sea. It was a spot well suited for romance of a certain kind: in the shadowy saloon, within the sound of the ocean, hearing the wind in the branches overhead, the hum of voices, and the beat of a small dance band, he felt relatively inconspicuous, and inclined to gaiety. Hildegarde's lessons were, fortunately, fresh in his mind: she had told him to try to believe that he was having a good time. "Sometimes," the charming basilisk had remarked, "if you are able to fool your companion, it even becomes possible to fool yourself. As far as the step is concerned, don't worry; you've seen the same dance performed over and over again beside the river Phlegethon, in the First Ring of the Sixth Circle, where those who have been violent against their neighbors do a twist of their own. Besides, you have only to remember the frantic hopping about which swept all Europe during the Middle Ages; it was called St. Vitus's dance, a nervous disorder, but then these are nervous times, or so they tell me.

"So . . . keep the right knee bent a little . . ."

Seated now beside Gladys Milhouser, the doctor-demon kept time with his feet under the table, and wondered how to start the conversation. "What shall it be?" he asked; "champagne?"

It was the only drink he knew, except brandy, which he considered a drink for men rather than for women. Besides, he remembered being told that champagne was always used in situations such as this; and that both gentlemen and demons had benefited from it.

Miss Milhouser had also heard about champagne, although she had never actually seen any. Her eyes sparkled, and she exclaimed enthusiastically:

"Hot dog!"

A moment later, realizing that she would be nineteen in a little over a year, and that she was the guest of a distinguished scientist at a night club, she amended her remark. "I mean," she declared demurely, "I'd love it."

The orchestra, a "small combo," was playing something which Samael took to be a waltz. "Shall we?" he inquired gravely, rising and taking hold of the back of her chair.

"I'd love it," she said again, and a moment later she was snuggled, as Beelzebub had foreseen, in Samael's arms.

But not for long. To Gladys, apparently, the music was not a waltz; rather, it was an invitation to perform. Samael found himself alone upon the floor, while Gladys circled around him, shaking her hips, waving her arms, and executing a series of steps which he had seen before in Africa and among the head-hunting tribes of New Guinea. Is it the twist? he thought in a panic, and tried to remember what Hildegarde had taught him.

It was not the twist; it was a form of the cha-cha. Gladys, still gyrating, approached and retreated, glided in and out of his arms, circled his neck, and appeared again from in back. When the music ended, she stood flushed and smiling, and reached for his hand. "That was really far out," she said. "Neato."

Samael smiled back at her. It amused him to think that he had been afraid she might feel too warm in his embrace.

The champagne was ready at their table, and Samael lost no time in filling Gladys' glass with the pale, lemon-yellow liquid. He disliked champagne himself, but he trusted to its power. "To my charming guest," he said, raising his glass.

Gladys took a sip and immediately made a face which she hastened to conceal behind an interested smile. "It's very nice," she said. And she added, trying to forget the taste of what she had just swallowed:

"This was really a wonderful idea."

"I'm afraid I am not a very good dancer," said Samael apologetically. "I've had so little opportunity . . ."

But Gladys insisted that on the contrary he was a divine dancer. "You're quiet," she said, "but you've got rhythm. I mean, you don't get in the way or anything. With most older people, they're always wanting to grab you. Like the way my father . . ."

She was suddenly silent, and her face became closed and secretive. "I take it," he said evenly, "that your father doesn't know where you are."

A slight blush stained the peach down of her face. "Not exactly," she admitted. "Anyway . . . what he doesn't know won't hurt him."

"I'm glad you feel that way about it," said Samael. "Because, you see, I need your help; in quite a private matter."

Curious, flushed, she gazed at him with parted lips. "Yes?" she breathed. "What do you want from me?"

"It's about Mr. Sneeden," Samael began.

Her face fell, and she began to rearrange the cutlery in front of her. "Oh for goodness' sakes," she sighed, "him again!"

She turned back with a look of infinite weariness. "I don't even know he's alive," she said. "Honestly."

"After all," said Samael obstinately, "he is a handsome young man. And he'd like to be your friend."

"I choose my own friends," said Gladys. "Okay?"

"If you would only give him a chance," said Samael in his most coaxing manner.

She looked at him through narrowed eyes, and with a curious expression. "Why do you keep talking about this Mr. Sneeden?" she asked. "What's it to you, what I think about him, anyway?"

"It is only that I have his interests at heart," murmured Samael. "He has confided in me."

To his dismay he saw her turn her face away from him, and the bright head bent in dejection. "I thought you liked me," she said in a small voice.

"Oh, but I do!" cried Samael. "Truly I do! I like you very much. And I hope that you like me."

Now why did I say that? he thought. He had an idea that Cyrano would have acted differently.

"I like you very much too," she said simply. "I thought you knew it."

"Thank you," he said unhappily. "But you see, I'm quite an elderly fellow . . ."

"Maybe I like older men," she murmured, and glanced up at him for a moment from under her lashes.

He gave what he hoped was a light laugh. "Surely," he protested, "not this much older!"

However, he realized that the moment had come. Leaning across the table, he placed his hand on hers. At once a fire ran through her veins and she gave a tiny gasp. Samael failed to hear it; he had his duty to perform, and only wished that he had brought Cyrano along with him.

He would simply have to do the best he could.

"My child," he said in his best voice, "you are so young! Enjoy your youth while you can. Lives were not meant to be hoarded, but to be given away in joy; the loveliest day in the world is one which has been handed to you by a friend or a stranger, without care, like a cup of water."

"From a friend or a stranger," echoed Gladys, gazing into his eyes. Smiling, she removed her hand from beneath his, and grasping her glass, lifted it in his direction.

"You're so right," she said.

He felt a sudden surge of triumph. "Then you'll go out with Alfred?" he asked. "To please me?"

"Alfred?" She made a face, pouting into her

glass. "Is that what you want me to do?"

"Yes," he said.

"I thought you said you liked me."

"I did. I do."

"Then why do you want me to date another man? Are you queer or something?"

"Certainly not!" said Samael. And he added unhappily:

"Aren't you afraid of me at all?"

She gave him a look, half tremulous, half mocking, across the edge of her glass. "I don't think you know very much about young girls nowadays, do you!" she said. "For a man of the world?"

"It has been a long time," Samael said, and retired into a depressed silence. But Gladys continued to gaze at him with eyes warm as summer, and swimming with speculation. When is he going to make a pass? she wondered. Or do I have to do it all myself?

The orchestra burst suddenly into the most raucous sound he had ever heard, and he started up in alarm, expecting to see all the hordes of hell, homely, familiar, and obscene, descend upon the room in billows of smoke and flame. But it was only the twist. And the startled demon watched in astonishment as the floor filled almost at once with dancing couples; with arms working like boxers, they glared into each other's eyes, swayed, churned, twisted, corkscrewed up and down, but never touched; now one and then the other seemed to gain a momentary ascendancy, only to lose it again. He realized that Gladys was trying to say something to him, for he saw her lips moving, but in the din he was unable to hear a word, and could only smile weakly back at her. It is the sound of Chaos, he thought, and I have heard it before, when Lucifer stormed the Gates of Heaven and was cast down, and all of us along with him.

He shuddered, and wished to flee. But to cross the floor would have been impossible, and it occurred to him that he had heard such sounds and watched such scenes still another time, in less fearful circumstances, and he looked anxiously at the wall for the hand to appear and to write:

Mene, Mene, Tekel Upharsin.

The dread words did not appear. Instead, in Beelzebub's handwriting, unseen by all but himself, there materialized on the ceiling the following adjuration:

"Get with it!"

CHAPTER 13

Who knows where chance leaves off and destiny takes over? The moment is a puff of dandelion seed, unnoticeable—or so terrible that the heart breaks . . . but mends itself again and turns in another direction. Alfred, on his way to deliver a repaired clock-radio to the Sebastian house, stopped his pickup truck in front of Scotti's Tavern long enough to hear a few bars of music in the cool night air, and to see Gladys come out of the front

entrance clinging to the arm of Dr. Hod and gazing up at him in a way which could not be misin-
terpreted.

The shock of it numbed him; and was followed
by a tempest of grief which shook him to his marrow. So that was it! That was why Gladys was indifferent to him—kept him at arm's length and
gave him those cold looks! The doctor, his doctor,
who had told him to leave everything to him. . . .
Alfred knew what that meant now; it meant leave
Gladys to him, too.

He had a moment of wanting to confront them,
accuse them—but his wrath and grief were too
much for him, and too much mixed with shame.
He had been fooled, cheated, sold out, and all in
the dark behind his back. His heart felt curiously
empty, and yet there was a weight in his chest; he
found it difficult to breathe. Bewildered, sick with
rage and mortification, he wrenched at the wheel,
jammed in the gears, and fled, his face twisted
with anguish.

"What on earth was that?" asked Gladys, clinging to her companion.

Samael, who knew only too well what it was, replied gravely: "I'm afraid it was still another mistake."

In this state, then, of despair, certain that he had been betrayed, but not sure by whom, Alfred arrived at Miss Sebastian's house—a house which had been left her by her parents, and which she used to rent out rooms, keeping only a parlor and bedroom for herself. The postmistress, who had just returned from her evening visit with Father Deener, opened the door herself, and after taking one look at Alfred's ravaged face, exclaimed:

"Mr. Sneeden! Whatever is the matter?"

To her consternation, Alfred began to weep. "I saw it," he said. "I seen it with my own eyes."

And he added in accents of despair:

"Everything is gone to Hell."

Miss Sebastian watched him gravely; she had never seen a man cry before, and the sight embarrassed her. "There," she said soothingly. "I'm sure it can't be that bad."

But a moment later, remembering her conversation with Father Deener, she had a premonition of the truth, and Alfred's mention of Hell failed to surprise her. "Tell me, Mr. Sneeden," she said firmly: "are you in trouble?"

He shook his head and blew his nose, which allowed her time to think; and after a moment or two, during which she debated with herself, she led him somewhat hesitantly into her parlor and sat him down on the old horsehair sofa which had belonged to her parents. "What you need," she said, "is a hot cup of tea."

"Thank you, ma'am," said Alfred meekly. He looked about him at his surroundings, and drew a long, dreary breath ending in a sigh. It was all so different from his own tumbledown quarters: the solid mahogany whatnot in its corner, full of china and small souvenirs, the walnut table with its fringed table-cover, the bookcase with its glass doors, the Boston rocker, the beaded lamps, the framed prints on the walls, Landseer's "Stag at Bay," and "The Doctor's Christmas Eve." It reminded him somehow of childhood and his mother's knee, though he himself had been brought up in far more modest circumstances. Despite himself, he felt vaguely comforted. "It's nice here," he said.

With the tea he seemed to relax. "You'll have to excuse me," he said, "coming in here and acting the way I did. I never did anything like that before. I guess it was from seeing my girl come out of that place with the doctor."

"Your girl?" asked Mary carefully.

He hung his head. "She was," he said; "or anyway, I thought she was. I had this agreement . . ."

His voice trailed off. "That's the way I understood it," he said doggedly.

An agreement? A pact, perhaps? Mary's heart skipped a beat. "With whom?" she asked, a little breathlessly. "I mean . . . what did you agree to?"

Alfred explained that he had contracted for a course of treatments to make him young again. "He's got this machine," he said, "that does it."

He looked down at himself with a sort of shy satisfaction. "It works, all right," he said. "Sometimes I hardly know myself."

"And this . . . this girl?"

He looked down and fiddled with his teacup. "What else would I do it for?" he asked.

She felt a little pang in her heart; it surprised her. It was true: what else did a man ever do a thing like that for? For a girl . . . for a woman. She was a woman, too—wasn't she? But no one ever did anything like that for her.

However, this was no time to think about herself. It all added up, she realized: it was just what Father Deener had suspected. "Did you sign anything?" she asked anxiously.

"We have this contract," he admitted, "between Doctor and I. It's like when you go to a hospital, you always have to sign something."

"But did you sign it?"

"Yes, ma'am; I was obliged to."

"You signed your soul away," said Mary with finality, and felt like crying.

"No, ma'am," said Alfred; "I didn't. It was my heart. They wanted it for research or something."

Mary asked him if he had a copy of the contract, but he told her no, he only got the treatments. "I go every day," he said, "and sit there in front of that little black box. I never see anybody else there, excepting Gladys . . . Miss Milhouser. I don't think Doctor has anybody but me, for a patient."

"That's all he needs," she said quietly.

"You think I did wrong?"

"Yes," she said. And she added with all the warmth of her womanly heart:

"You poor man!"

Alfred was touched, but at the same time he felt confused. He hadn't thought of himself as someone to be pitied, and he wasn't ready for it. "I don't know," he said uncertainly: "how come he'd have an office like that, with all those diplomas on the walls, if it was wrong?

"Besides, what good would my heart do me, after I was done with it?"

"After you were done with it," she repeated. "And when would that be?"

"When I'm dead," he said cheerlessly.

"What makes you so sure?" she asked.

Alfred felt a first, slight moment of alarm. He realized that no definite time limit had been set; but Dr. Hod had assured him that they were in no hurry. He wondered, for the first time, who "they" were.

She sat thinking, wrinkling her brow. "There's only one person can help you," she said: "Father Deener."

"A priest?" asked Alfred in surprise. "What would I want a priest for?"

"It's because he is a priest," said Mary.

"Listen," said Alfred: "it's just an understanding

between a doctor and I. That's all. I wouldn't want to go see a priest about a thing like that."

But just the same, he was vaguely uneasy; he kept thinking about that night on the hill in back of Gladys' house, when he had said . . . what had he said? He couldn't remember. Had he said something about his soul? He didn't think so; and all that had happened was that he'd caught a cold. His soul still belonged to him, as far as he knew: no one had even asked for it.

And as for Gladys . . . he hadn't gotten her, either.

He realized that for a little while he hadn't been thinking about her. With the return of memory came that empty feeling in his heart again; and suddenly he felt very lonely. He would have liked to stay a little longer in the homely, old-fashioned room, but he knew that it was time to go. "I certainly appreciate your interest," he said, rising to his feet. "It's been a real pleasure."

She followed him to the door. "Please go to see

Father Deener," she said. "I know that he'll be glad
to see you."

"Well, maybe I will someday, at that," he said.

He looked back once as he drove away. She
stood in the doorway watching him, a friendly and
somehow comforting figure. "Drive carefully," she
called after him. "Take care."

"Yes, ma'am," he said. "I will."

CHAPTER 14

It was too late that night for Mary to reach Father Deener. Hurrying to church early the next morning, she found the old priest sweeping out the sacristy. Laying aside his broom and dustrag, the good and kindly man led the postmistress out of doors into the sunlight. "What is it, my child?" he asked gently; "you do not usually come to see me so early in the morning."

"I came to tell you that you were right," she exclaimed; "Mr. Sneeden is a lost soul."

Father Deener was not surprised, having already come to the same conclusion, but he was a little astonished to hear her admit that she felt a good deal of sympathy for him. "He did it for love," she said.

"That is the usual reason," remarked Father Deener drily.

"Is it wrong," asked Mary anxiously, "for me to be sorry for him, and to want to help him?"

"It is your duty," replied Father Deener firmly. "But remember, the Devil has many resources at his command, and many devious ways to ensnare and to entrap, and pity is very powerful and sometimes leads to disaster. I am thinking of the monk Paphnutius, who pitied the courtesan Thais and succeeded in saving her, only to discover too late that what he took to be pity was in fact a different emotion altogether. Save him if you can, as a Christian; but be careful not to lose in the meanwhile anything that could not be replaced."

While this conversation was going on outside the church, to the accompaniment of birdsong and the faraway, low rumble of the sea, Samael, seated among the bushes by the side of Mrs. Mc-Henry's pool, was talking things over with Beelzebub, who, in the guise of an inflated swan, floated peacefully nearby in the water, or propelled by the breeze, approached the bank in graceful swoops. "You have only yourself to blame for last night," said Beelzebub; "a more inept seduction I have never seen."

And in scornful tones, he exclaimed:

"Cyrano, indeed!"

"At least," said Samael, "Cyrano was able to use the mails. He didn't have to spend an evening with Roxanne in Scotti's Tavern. I assure you, the joint was fairly jumping."

"What a vocabulary," said Beelzebub admiringly.

"Besides," Samael went on plaintively, "he was in love with the girl. Whereas I . . ."

"Yes?" asked Beelzebub.

It was impossible for Samael to blush, but for a moment a bluish flame, as from gas, seemed to play about his features. "What do you take me for?" he murmured.

Beelzebub managed to shrug his wings. "You weren't so choosy in the old days," he remarked. " 'And it came to pass when men began to multiply on the face of the earth, and daughters were born to them, that the sons of God saw the daughters of men that they were fair . . .' "

"I know, I know," said Samael testily; "you needn't remind me. I was younger then."

He mused for a moment, not without regret. "I was telling Matilda about it only a few days ago," he said.

"Women were women in those days," said Beelzebub with a sigh. "There was none of this modern nonsense about women's rights."

A puff of wind drove him momentarily toward the opposite end of the pool; however, by a series of brilliantly executed tacks he managed to regain his own side again. "Who is Matilda?" he asked.

"She is an ant," replied Samael, "and I have thought lately that we could do worse than to woo these tiny insects, who, although anonymous in their personal lives, have great force and power when acting as a community."

Beelzebub looked thoughtful. "You know that we are up to our necks in communities," he said, "and besides, I believe that Lucifer leans to cockroaches."

"Ants," remarked Samael, "are a perfect example of the welfare state. They believe in conformity, and in security. Whereas the cockroach is an individual. With the cockroaches it would be the same thing as before: we'd have to win them one at a time. Whereas with the ants, it would be the Third Reich all over again; they would all come marching happily into Hell, led by their soldiers."

"The Third Reich," said Beelzebub, "was not a welfare state."

At this point an indignant voice sounded from

the grass at Samael's feet, and looking down, he observed Matilda and the large ant with several of their relatives. "We are not National Socialists," said the large ant, and Matilda added:

"To each according to his need; from each according to his ability. We offer the world peace, freedom, and the benefit of the people's democracy." To which the large ant responded proudly:

"We will bury the cockroaches and anyone else who opposes us."

Beelzebub looked at Samael thoughtfully. "My friend," he said, "I think you have something."

And with a flirt of his wings he gave a little pirouette in the water.

"The only question is: do they have souls?"

Samael looked questioningly at Matilda, who fiddled with her front legs in a gesture of uncertainty. "After all," said Samael, "did Australopithecus have a soul? It is a difficult question. Adam knew his Creator; they used to walk in the Garden together. And Cain knew Him; the All-High gave that impetuous fellow a distinguishing mark so that no one would hurt him. But after Cain, nobody seems to have known Him until Enos."

He chewed on his finger. "I am trying to remember," he said uncomfortably, "what we were doing all that time."

"Housekeeping," said Beelzebub comfortably. "Setting up our new quarters. Repairing the banks of Acheron, marking the limits of Limbo, dredging the Styx, broadening Phlegethon, building the gates of Dis, laying out the seventeen Circles and the ten Malebolge, digging the Well . . . we were quite busy, as a matter of fact."

Samael nodded his head. "I remember," he said. "Limbo was dreadfully crowded. But after Enos, the Circles began to fill."

Looking down, he observed a certain commotion among the ants at his feet, and what appeared to be confusion or distress on Matilda's part. Upon asking her what was the matter, he received the following reply:

"When we spoke to you last, you told us about love and about the heart: it was interesting, if not altogether instructive, and we went home and gave it some thought; it is presently before the Central Committee as part of their regular business. But now you talk about the soul, which, like love, is a term we do not understand. We have never felt the presence of this organ in our bodies, which are armored to withstand the most furious assaults. In what portion would the soul be located? Under the thorax, or in the abdomen? And why, if you ask us for our hearts, do you demand our souls as well . . . that is, supposing that we have any?"

"Allow me," said Beelzebub, drifting as close to the bank as possible. "I believe I can explain."

After a moment's reflection, he spoke as follows:

"Long, long ago life developed upon this planet in the warm shallows of the sea. Nurtured by salts and chemicals, and by the rays of the sun, the first cells grew and, being both male and female, divided and multiplied; before long new forms appeared, due to radiations from space and waves of energy let loose by earthquakes, volcanos, lightning storms, hurricanes, tornadoes, and other phenomena. Soon the sea, and then the land, was filled with living forms, both animals and vegetable.

"Eons later there appeared on earth through mutation, natural selection, survival of the fittest, and the direct intervention of the Most High, a creature called man. This was on the sixth day, sidereally speaking. He was not as graceful as the gazelle, as brave as the eagle, as strong as ivy, as gentle as the May fly, or as beautiful as a crocus, but he had something no other creature had: he was capable of development. Within that hairy and, upon the whole, defenseless body there rested a brain fitted for abstract thought, and a heart able to feel that concentration of rapture, of longing and delight, of hunger and gentleness, affection, kindness, jealousy, anguish, and worship which we call love. And because there was room in it for worship, man also grew a soul—at what point in his development, no one knows. As Samael has pointed out, we were not watching too carefully at the time.

"The question of whether or not you, my small friends, can be said to have souls at this point is academic: the important thing is whether you have hearts. Because, if you do, there is room for the soul to develop, as in the case of Australopithecus."

"We have hearts," replied the larger ant firmly. "They beat for the whole insect world, except spiders, ant lions, termites, centipedes, cockroaches, stinkbugs, and other ants. And if what we feel for aphids and certain household bugs whom we have accepted as pets can be called love, then perhaps as you say we have the beginnings of a soul.

"However, we cannot give you our souls separately, you must take all or nothing. And there must be some reciprocity, such as favored treatment in the sugar bowl, where we have to compete with flies, mites, beetles, and sudden discouraging disappearances.

"But first of all, we must be allowed to bury the cockroaches."

A few inches away, and out of sight, a small cockroach parted the grass out of sight of the ants, who were awaiting Beelzebub's reply. "Our security is threatened," the cockroach exclaimed, as he scurried off, "but I am sure that the same sterling virtues which enabled us to survive for hundreds of millions of years will keep us from being buried tomorrow. So then—every cockroach for himself! The desire for liberty is basic, and can never be wholly eradicated from the insect heart.

"At the same time, it would be wise to look for a leader to tell us what to think."

CHAPTER 15

The cockroach was not the only one to overhear these conversations; Delia McHenry, peering from her window, saw the town's new doctor, Dr. Hod, talking to her swan, and the bird, apparently, replying. Their voices carried in a low murmur across the garden to her room, although she was unable to understand a single syllable of what they were saying. Shaken and terrified, she felt that her heart was about to beat through the cage of her chest, or else stop altogether; and with a frozen motion she put down the bottle of Old Fitzgerald which she had just taken from its hiding place under the bed.

It was then that Delia McHenry swore never to touch another drop of liquor as long as she lived.

When Mr. McHenry arrived home that evening, he found the swan as usual floating silent and motionless upon the surface of the pool, and Mrs. McHenry asleep, having been given a sedative by Dr. Fleming, as well as a shot of vitamin B_1, hot milk, and a sleeping pill.

Samael, meanwhile, had gone to speak to Alfred, whom he found in a sullen and obstinate mood. The demon knew better than to waste time in apologies, and adopting a severe tone, exclaimed:

"I am disappointed in you."

He went on to say that time was running out, and that he would have to ask for his payment; to which Alfred replied in a voice trembling with outrage:

"You said that you were in no hurry. You said that I could keep it until I was done with it."

"It seems to me," said Samael coldly, "that you are already done with it. You have not succeeded with Miss Milhouser; what good is your heart to you if no one wants it?"

"I want it," said Alfred; but he was frightened.

"That doesn't count," replied Samael, unmoved. And he added: "I was quite willing to wait, in order to help you out—but since you have so obviously failed in your designs, I do not see the point of waiting any longer.

"I also have my orders, and am obliged to work more or less on schedule."

"If I've failed," said Alfred bitterly, "it's been your doing. I saw you last night . . . the two of you!"

"I know you did," said Samael calmly. "I also know that you went to Miss Sebastian's house, and enjoyed a cup of tea."

Alfred's jaw dropped. "How do you know that?" he stammered. "Who told you?"

Samael shrugged his shoulders. "Does it matter?" he asked. "Let's just say that I know more than you think. Among the things I know is the fact that the postmistress is attracted to you—although she herself is not yet aware of it—and that Miss Milhouser is not. She is, unfortunately, attracted to me, although I did nothing to encourage her, and am far too old for her anyhow. Or perhaps she is too old for me: I have, if anything, a liking for twelve-year-olds. They have such a delicious perversity, for they have not yet resigned themselves to their sex, and are full of curiosity, resentment, and guilt. Not all of them, of course; there have been some twelve-year-olds who have made us . . . who have made me . . . very uncomfortable. I am thinking of Thérèse Martin, and Bernadette Soubirous, both of whom were invincible. And there were others.

"In any event, your Miss Milhouser frightens me. She tells me that I do not understand the modern young woman, and she is right. I was brought up with the double standard, and I am frank to say that I am uncomfortable with any other."

"Well," said Alfred obstinately, "you can't have my heart, and that's that. Not yet. Not until I've had one more try at it."

"By all means," agreed Samael; "try again; a little harder this time. Put your heart into it." He allowed himself a wintry smile. "And in the meanwhile," he said, "come around for another treatment in the morning. I am very punctilious about my obligations.

"After all—a contract is a contract."

That same night, Gladys, leaning from her window, her soft round elbows on the sill, swung her hair idly to and fro, dreaming and smiling at the stars. The odors of earth, the fragrance of flowers and trees surrounded her, and in the shadows she imagined that the blossoms were unfolding, holding out their arms to her in joy. At the same time she felt a delicious sadness, and the sensation of no longer belonging to herself. She had no appetite.

Had her grandmother been alive, old Mrs. Milhouser would have called it the green-sickness. Gladys preferred to believe that she was in love. Framed in the golden lamplight, she appeared to Alfred, watching in the shadows, more beautiful than ever, as she leaned, bemused, in his direction, repeating in musical tones:

> *"Starlight, star bright,*
> *Very first star I see tonight,*
> *Wish I may, wish I might*
> *Have the wish I wish tonight."*

Her wish was simple: it was to be folded in Dr. Hod's arms, to be swept off her feet, and to enjoy with him those ultimate delights which she had occasionally heard about, and of which she had had a few unsatisfactory samples in the rear seats of cars or behind the bushes at school dances. She wished to triumph over Sally Ewart and Henry Muggins, and to experience a breath-taking romance with the most romantic figure in town; and even, perhaps—though she was not at all sure, there being such a difference in their ages—to become Mrs. Samuel Hod.

So, when Alfred stepped suddenly out of the shadows with outstretched arms and a hoarse cry, she gave him one outraged look, and exclaimed:

"Get lost!"

And added, before she slammed the window shut:

"Okay?"

He was lost, as he indeed knew. Humiliated, rejected, and doubly damned, he stumbled away in the darkness, not knowing or caring where. He kept waiting for the awful sorrow to hit him, the full grief to weigh down his heart . . . but it felt surprisingly light. His anguish seemed all in his head.

He was not, perhaps, as much surprised as he was relieved to find himself once more in front of Mary Sebastian's modest house, and to have her open the door and invite him in. And once again he sat in the little parlor, on the horsehair sofa, holding a cup of tea.

She had been secretly hoping that he would call on her, but seeing him there so soon again threw her into a flutter. She was confused; at one moment shuddering at finding herself in such close proximity to the powers of darkness, and the next filled with a sort of evangelical fervor and the determination to save him. The only thing she had not expected was to find herself jealous of Gladys Milhouser. And when Alfred, over his teacup, gave her a stricken look which, however, seemed to have no actual pain behind it, she was unable to contain herself any longer, and declared:

"I think you have been very badly treated."

"So do I," agreed Alfred soberly. " 'A contract is a contract,' he says. But where's my share of it, I'd like to know?"

"Of course," she began comfortingly, "you do look unusually well."

"I had my heart set on a certain beauty in the

town," declared Alfred. "But she turned me down. That's not the way I heard the story told."

"I know," said Mary. "It was Marguerite."

"That's right," said Alfred: "Marguerite. Only her name is Gladys."

He looked at the postmistress with sudden curiosity. "How did you find out about Marguerite?" he demanded. "Before, when I asked you, you said you didn't know."

"So you remember that," said Mary. "I didn't know which one you meant," she explained apologetically.

She was silent for a moment, stirring her tea. "Gladys," she said at last: "Gladys Milhouser. That child. I never really thought of her as a beauty. Pretty, yes . . . but beautiful?"

Alfred sighed deeply. "The queer thing about it is," he said, "I don't feel much. Not like what you'd expect. I'm like you might say, numb. Only it's more like I was empty, if you know what I mean. As if my heart . . ."

He turned suddenly pale, and put his hand to his breast. "You don't think they've taken it already?" he asked fearfully.

But in another moment he relaxed and sat back slumped in his chair. "It's still there," he said. "I could feel it beating."

Nevertheless, Mary was alarmed. Perhaps, she thought, they are taking it little by little. And when they have taken the whole of it, he will wake up some day without any heart at all. But then, her thoughts ran on, he'll be dead! And she was immediately overwhelmed with grief.

Surprised at the violence of her own feelings, and moved by an unexpected impulse, she reached across the tea-table and clasped his hand in hers. "You mustn't die," she breathed. "I won't let you!"

Alfred found himself shaking. To die? So soon? It came as a distinct shock, for he had forgotten all about it. And he too, moved by fright and by an unknown emotion, rose suddenly to his feet, threw himself on his knees beside her, clasped her around the waist, and buried his face in her lap.

He was at once surprised by the softness of Miss Sebastian's body, the fragrance of her clothes, and the warmth and security of his resting place. "Save me," he murmured into the folds of material under which he could make out the gentle contours of her thighs. He was reminded of his childhood at his mother's knee, but with a difference; and for the first time it occurred to him that there still might be something to live for.

As for Mary, her hand, resting upon Alfred's head, clutched a little of his hair, and she had time to think that she must get him to stop putting oil on it. On her face, which he could not see, there was an expression of tenderness, and terror: tenderness because she too saw herself for a moment as a mother; and terror because she was aware of feelings within herself that she had never experienced before.

She thought that she would be able to control them. She was mistaken.

CHAPTER 16

The most Reverend "Rowdy" Fenston, Diocesan Bishop of Rockford, a see which embraced Parish, seven counties, and the capital city of the state, looked quietly at the old priest who stood before him. Father Deener's cassock was clean, but frayed and worn, and his face expressed humility, obedience, and resolution. Bishop Fenston, who had once played right tackle for Notre Dame, had

known Father Deener for a long time, and believed
that he understood him. He is like a child in a fairy
story, he thought, where even the dragons are
real. But from this strangely innocent and trustful
priest arises an aroma of piety which fills me with
envy.

And with a gentle smile he remarked: "Do you
really believe that Satan himself is among us?"

Father Deener replied unequivocally that he
did. "Since we believe that he exists," he declared,
"and is present in human affairs, why should we
be surprised to discover him in person?"

And he narrated again the events leading up to
his determination to seek help from his superior.
"It is a fact," he remarked, "that the Devil appeared as a doctor in the past, and I am only astonished that I did not recognize him sooner."

Bishop Fenston sighed. "Father," he said, "we
are not living in the past. One might say that our
Blessed Lord is also present in men's affairs. But
we do not know Him, and so we do not always

believe it. We do not expect to see Him walking down the street, or entering the coffee shop at the corner."

"It would not surprise me in the least," said Father Deener. And he added earnestly:

"We must believe in what we cannot see, otherwise we must lose the argument to the scientists."

"Ah, yes," said the Bishop good-naturedly, "the scientists. But the Church has more things on her mind these days than theological discussions. Those of us who administer her affairs are concerned with her image in the public eye. The days of the great Doctors of the Church—of Hilary, of Augustine, of Thomas Aquinas, Gregory, Jerome —are long past: the voices which now command our admiration speak for the most part in French. It is no longer a matter of urgency to correct or discourage heresy: we are more concerned with the picture we present to the world. It should appear neither too liberal nor too conservative, neither too broad nor too narrow, but offering comfort and hope to all, which is in fact the definition of the word 'catholic,' or 'whole.'

"Not too long ago, the image of God was fixed: He presented a fatherly appearance, with a beard streaked with silver and eyes from which darted the lightnings of wrath, but which also brimmed with the dews of compassion. This view has been altered, due to the work of the biologists and chemists, with the result that God has become amorphous and is having a fierce struggle to keep from being confused with hydrogen. At such a moment, for the Church to assert that Satan is practicing medicine in the next town might very well draw down upon us the charge of medievalism, and alienate the sympathies of our best thinkers, or at least those who have gone beyond junior high."

Father Deener replied:

"If Satan appeared in the desert to Our Blessed Lord, he can just as easily appear on the main street of Parish, U.S.A."

Bishop Fenston bit his lip. He realized that he was caught in the old snare: if he denied Satan's appearance in the past, he thereby impugned the Gospels; if he admitted it, he was obliged to admit Father Deener's thesis as well. There had been no such problems on the football fields of Notre Dame.

"Supposing you are mistaken?" he said slowly. "Supposing this doctor is merely a harmless quack? We can scarcely afford to make a mistake of that sort."

Father Deener replied with dignity: "The Church, which persecuted Galileo, has survived its mistakes. It is the duty of the Apostolic Church to oppose the powers of darkness wherever they may appear.

"Besides," he added sensibly, "what quack wants a heart for his fee?"

"Don't tell me what my duty is," said the Bishop testily. "I am only too well aware of it myself. My duty is to keep order among the shepherds of my flock. The Prince of Darkness is, I think, adequately opposed by the Princes of the Church, including His Holiness, the Pope."

"In Parish?" asked Father Deener. And with a shining face, he exclaimed:

"I am only one of those same lowly shepherds whom you mentioned. But my staff is a shepherd's staff, stout, and with a crook in the handle. If I see a wolf among my sheep, I cry 'Wolf!' and if no one comes, I must wade in and battle the beast by myself, or be unworthy of the trust reposed in me."

"By whom?" asked the Bishop quietly.

Father Deener flushed. "By my Master," he replied bravely.

The Bishop gazed at him bleakly. "I suppose," he said wryly, "that you are not speaking of your ecclesiastical superior?"

"No, Your Excellency," said Father Deener; "I was not."

"I didn't think so," said the Bishop. "You know, of course," he continued, "that your stand smacks of heresy. The Catholic Church is a monolithic institution, no matter what anyone says to the contrary; and the threat of excommunication is no less terrible for its being used all too infrequently. Still, to be cast out, to be banished from the love and pity of God, is surely the most dreadful punishment, and that is why the Church is very sparing in its use. Nevertheless, the priest who sets himself up as his own arbiter in spiritual matters stands a good chance of falling into mortal error. The sin of pride, Father . . ."

"Like Joan of Arc?" asked Father Deener.

"Like Joan of Arc," replied the Bishop steadily.

"She was pronounced Blessed," said Father Deener.

"Four hundred and seventy-eight years later," said the Bishop. "Twenty-five of them in Hell, and the rest of them in Limbo, until she was beatified. It was one of those unavoidable mistakes: technically, she was guilty, until proven innocent. It is the chance most martyrs take."

"Nevertheless," declared Father Deener obstinately, "I should like to try."

"To try what?" asked the Bishop, who had begun to lose track of the conversation.

"To drive Satan out of my parish!" exclaimed Father Deener.

The Bishop heaved a deep sigh. "I trust you'll be able to get him to go back to where he came from," he said drily. "I shouldn't care to find him parading around Rockford."

"That is not very likely, Your Excellency," said Father Deener tactfully; "he knows you would be too much for him."

The Bishop smiled faintly. He was tired of the argument, which seemed to him to be getting nowhere, but he knew when he was being flattered. The Devil indeed! he thought wryly; as though there wasn't enough trouble in the world! Still— Satan could take any form he chose: even that of a peddler of nostrums. "What do you want me to do?" he asked wearily. "Shall I come to Parish with you?"

"No, Your Excellency," said Father Deener promptly; "your appearance in Parish would arouse a certain amount of curiosity. We'd have reporters, and questions would be asked; the truth might come out, which could easily lead to panic."

"Well, then?" asked the Bishop.

"I should like permission to do this myself," said Father Deener.

Bishop Fenston sat back in relief. At least, he thought, he wouldn't have to make a fool of himself either by going to Parish or to the Cardinal. "Very well," he said, "I give you permission. Do you think you know how to go about it?"

"It is all in the Ritual," said Father Deener. "I intend to study it."

Bishop Fenston held out his hand for Father Deener to kiss the episcopal ring. It was his way of ending the audience. "You have my blessing, Father," he said in a kindly tone. "Let me know what happens."

CHAPTER 17

Father Deener returned to Parish and at once set about arranging a meeting between himself and Dr. Hod, whom he believed to be Satan in disguise. Encountering Miss Olney in the street, he asked her if she would take a note to the doctor, whose office was not far from her shop. Miss Olney turned pale, shuddered, and without replying hurried away to put something between her and the world.

The priest then wrote a note to Dr. Hod, inviting him to church the following day. "You may be surprised that I have chosen the church as a meeting place," he wrote, "but I hope that you will consider it a challenge worthy of an affirmative reply."

He received the reply the next day, delivered by Miss Milhouser. "My dear Father Deener," Samael wrote in a fine Spencerian hand, "I should be delighted to meet you for what I know you have in mind, but not in church, where I fear I should be somewhat outnumbered. Let me suggest, instead, that we meet at dusk tomorrow beside Mrs. McHenry's pool. The McHenrys, as you doubtless know, are all three of them gone on an extended holiday to the Islands, and we shall be quite alone, except, of course, for those ethereal legions who will be watching from the side lines."

And realizing that further concealment was useless, he signed his own name with a flourish:

"Samael, of Hod."

Father Deener spent that day and the next either in his study or in church on his knees. He had no doubt of his own charism—the touch of God's Hand upon his spirit—but he recognized his weakness, which was that same ignorance in which he took so much joy and which accepted a world of mysteries beyond his comprehension. "Shield me, great Angel," he prayed, kneeling before the statue of St. Michael, "from my own open-mindedness."

Promptly at dusk on the appointed day Father Deener could be seen making his way alone to the McHenry house, where, as Samael had predicted, he found no one at home. Entering through the garden gate, which he found unlocked, he approached the pool in silence. He carried with him a pinch of salt, and a bottle of holy water which had been blessed by the Bishop; and he held his Crucifix firmly in his hand. As he drew near the pool, he saw the swan floating quietly on its surface, and a moment later Samael rose from among the shadows along the bank, and greeted him. "Welcome, Father," he said, holding out his hand; "I have been waiting for you."

"You are Satan, are you not?" asked Father

Deener simply, ignoring the outstretched hand, but gazing with respect at this demon, who, in the dusk, beside the pool, seemed imbued with a majesty he had not noticed before.

Samael smiled, and made a gesture which struck Father Deener as inconclusive. "Yes," he said; "and yet, in a sense, no. That is to say, I am an emanation of Lucifer, that great Archangel, who is himself an emanation of the Most High; as are Michael, Gabriel, and Raphael."

"What?" cried Father Deener, surprised. "You dare to mention God?"

Samael gazed at him patiently in the gathering twilight. "Why not?" he asked gently. "We are His enemies, it is true; but we are also His angels, and necessary to Him as He is to us. We sometimes speak of Him as You-know-who, but that is left-over from the old days when His name consisted of four Hebrew letters and was never to be uttered."

He continued musingly: "You are right to fear

us and to distrust us. And yet, had it not been for
Satan, there would be no Catholic Church. Adam
and Eve in the Garden, dwelling together in innocence, immortal, untouched by passion or desire,
ignorant of guilt, would have had no need of the
confessional."

"That is true," Father Deener replied. "And God
would not have been obliged to send His only-begotten Son to ransom mankind. Jesus upon the
Cross has Satan to thank for the vinegar and the
gall."

Samael frowned and bit his lip. "You have a
point, Father," he admitted. "But do not forget
that we were at war with Heaven. And all's fair
in . . ."

"Indeed," cried Father Deener indignantly, "all
is not fair at all! Most of the world's anguish has
come from those words, which were surely invented by the Devil!"

"You are weak in your history, Father," said
Samael coldly. "Do you think it was Satan who

told the Israelites to borrow silver and jewels from their Egyptian friends, who trusted them, the night before the Passover? It was not Satan, Father! Nor was one of us with Gideon at the well of Harod."

"Why do you keep harping on the past?" exclaimed Father Deener in vexed tones. "Are you acquainted only with the Old Testament?"

Samael shrugged his shoulders. "God is God," he said, "equally in the past as in the present; although in the later writings He has been marvelously gentled. If I go back more often to the Old Testament than to the New, it is because we demons are Semitic in origin: in those early days when we assumed the forms of men we naturally took on the features of those who saw and feared us. Would Jacob have worshipped a Hottentot? So too the Hosts of Heaven, whose angels showed themselves to the Jews as other Jews, winged and immortal; nothing else would do. We exist, Father, because God made us, as He made you; but you see us as you imagine us to be, and we assume the only guise by which you can recognize us, the guise of a man. An ant sees us as an ant.

"However—we have talked long enough, I think. Shall we proceed with the exorcism?"

"By all means!" said Father Deener. Sprinkling a little holy water on the ground, he advanced a step toward Samael, holding his Crucifix before him. "Avaunt, Satan!" he exclaimed. "Depart from this place, in the name of the Father, the Son, and the Holy Ghost!"

Samael nodded his head encouragingly. "Go on, Father," he said. "Let us hear the whole thing. That little bit would scarcely have served the Gadarene swine."

Somewhat daunted, but gripping his Crucifix all the tighter, Father Deener sprinkled more water around him in a circle, and after making the Sign of the Cross, repeated in a firm voice:

"*In nomine Jesu Christi Dei et Domini nostri, intercedente immaculata Virgine Dei Genetrice*

Maria, Beato Michaele Archangelo, beatis Apostolis Petro et Paulo et omnibus Sanctis, et sacra ministerii nostri auctoritate confisi, ad infestationes diabolicae fraudis repellendas securi aggredimur!"

He stopped for breath, to find Samael apparently unmoved, regarding him with what almost seemed like affection. "Lord, Lord," Father Deener prayed, shutting his eyes tight, "help me! Strengthen my spirit; harden my resolve. Let me feel again upon my parched spirit the dew of grace!"

"Get along with it, Father," said Samael gently: "there is still a great deal to come."

"Have you no fear, demon?" asked the priest in a shaking voice.

Samael smiled in the darkness which had by this time descended on the garden. About them the frogs shrilled and crickets rang their little bells, while above their heads the quiet stars shone down. And on the calm surface of the water the rubber swan floated gently to and fro, occasionally—or so it seemed to the disturbed priest—cocking a sardonic eye at the two duelists who confronted each other without wavering.

Father Deener took a deep breath. *"Exorcizamus te,"* he cried, *"omnis immunde spiritus, omnis satanica potestas, omnis incursio infernalis adversarii, omnis legio, omnis congregatio et secta diabolica, in nomine et virtute Domini nostri Jesu"*— here he made the Sign of the Cross—*"Christi, eradicare et effugare a Dei Ecclesia ab animabus ad imaginem Dei conditis ac pretioso divini Agni sanguine redemptis"*—

Again he made the Sign of the Cross. "Dare go no further, audacious serpent," he exclaimed, "to deceive the human race!"

"It is beautiful, Father," said Samael quietly, "but it is useless. It is too old-fashioned: it belongs to a more innocent time in history, when good and evil were easily separated into black and white. It is not so simple any more."

Father Deener bowed his head. "I know," he said.

Samael continued: "In those days, when the

great Cathedrals were being built, faith was a mighty bastion, and piety a terrible weapon before which our spirits quailed. We were wounded by men's obstinate longing for God's grace, and recoiled before their sublime belief in His goodness. Things are different today; we are no longer feared and hated; on the contrary, evil is debated, studied, and pronounced a natural cause. And as we have grown stronger, the walls of faith have weakened and begun to crumble, and piety that was once a sword aimed at our hearts has been blunted and allowed to rust. And who has done all this, Father? Lucifer? Satan? No, my friend; it has been man himself.

"He has learned much; he stands today upon the very threshold of the great mysteries. But they will not make him innocent again, or fill him with that grace which gave his spirit strength, or make him happy. Of all the gifts given him at the beginning, what has he left? Tell me."

The priest was silent for a moment. At last he said in a low voice:

"He has the gift of love."

"Yes," said Samael slowly, "he has the gift of love. But can he love beyond himself?"

"He has loved God," said Father Deener. "And that is beyond himself."

Samael winced, but refused to admit defeat. "Has it been without thought of gain?" he asked. "Or did he seek salvation?" And drawing himself up to his full height, he demanded:

"Can he love me?"

And for a single instant, while the earth shook and the stars were blotted out in the sky, he showed himself to Father Deener in all the power and the majesty of evil.

The old priest was not frightened, and gazed back at him unmoved. Samael was surprised. "You are not shaken, Father?" he asked. "How can that be?"

"You have not shown me anything I have not already seen in man," said Father Deener sadly.

CHAPTER 18

Father Deener left the McHenry house with a profound sense of failure and an infinite weariness. He had no desire to return to his study lined with books or to sit in his own garden beneath the trees; instead he made his way with slow steps down the path which led to the sea. There, seated upon a boulder, he gazed out at the immensity of the night, in which, far off, millions of years away, the rim of his own universe, powdered with stars, wheeled on its milky way through space.

The waves rising out of the darkness broke on the shore in sudden lines of foam. The cool sea-wind bathed his face still fevered from the encounter with the demon, and little by little, he felt himself grow quiet and resigned. It is true, he thought: eternity is all around us; we are in it, and yet we cannot see it. We cannot see God, either. Yet I can love the silent night and the heavens lit by stars whose size I cannot measure, and whose distance, one from another, is beyond imagining. And so I should love God; and so I do love Him, though all I have ever seen of Him is this world beneath my feet and the heavens overhead.

For we walk by faith, and not by sight. That is the human condition.

A star fell, for a brief moment penciling a streak of silver across the sky. And Father Deener reflected on how little men knew about the universe in which their planet moved like a tiny moon

[*181*]

around its sun, which itself, of no great size, whirled on its way across vast stretches of the cosmos, from nowhere to nowhere. One cannot believe, he said, that nothing guides its course; or that it would have been impossible for God to have dictated parts of the Old Testament.

Comforted by these thoughts, he gazed around him more cheerfully and noticed for the first time that he was not alone on the beach. The figure of a woman was seated, like himself, upon a rock a short distance away. Father Deener rose to leave, but as he passed near her he saw that it was the postmistress, Mary Sebastian. "My dear friend," he exclaimed in alarm, "whatever are you doing here all alone, so late at night?"

"Is it you, Father?" asked Mary. She seemed to have been weeping, and kept her gaze on the sand at her feet. "I've been thinking," she said in a low voice, not looking up.

Father Deener let himself down onto the rock beside her, and clasped his hands around his knees.

"So have I," he said. "And I have decided that I am only a foolish old man, and not St. Michael after all."

Mary's hands were folded in her lap. "And I," she said, "am only a foolish old woman and not any saint at all."

And with a sigh she added:

"What is it like to be in love, Father?"

Father Deener hesitated before replying. "To tell you the truth," he said at last, "I do not know. I should imagine that there would be a feeling of great joy attached to it."

"Yes," said Mary doubtfully. "And grief? A sudden rush of sorrow?"

"Why, I suppose so," said the priest. "I should think it very likely. All mortal flesh must turn to dust; and so the loving spirit grieves, being already bereft, in imagination."

"And wanting to die?" asked Mary. "For the sake of . . . of the other person?"

"The wish to sacrifice oneself for the beloved is

fairly common, I believe," said Father Deener.

"Sometimes," said Mary in a faraway voice, "I feel like singing; and then again, at other times, like crying."

"That is also the human condition," said Father Deener.

Turning, she clasped the old priest's hands in both of hers and peered anxiously into his face.

"Oh, Father," she cried, "what am I to do?"

Father Deener patted her hands reassuringly, but after a moment he stopped and looked away. "I was unable to get rid of the demon," he said. "Poor Mr. Sneeden; he has had no help from me, I'm afraid."

It was Mary's turn to console him. "Never mind," she said bravely. "I'm sure you did all you could."

But she turned silent after that, and sat for a while motionless in the dark. "Each day his heart grows lighter and emptier," she said at last. "There'll come a day when there is no more heart left at all."

She gave a little cry. "I can't bear to think of it," she said.

Father Deener sighed. How often, he thought sadly, a woman's heart seems to fasten upon an unworthy or unlikely object. And a momentary feeling of jealousy invaded his own heart, to realize that the companion of his evening walks in the garden no longer thought of him first. It lasted no more than a minute, and he put it aside with shame; it was not only selfish, but unrealistic. And not wishing to hurt her feelings, he contented himself with a few reassuring sounds. "Of course," he murmured; "naturally. That is to say . . .

"If you love him . . ."

"But that's just it," cried Mary; "do I? I don't know. That is . . . I think; how can I? And then, when he touches me . . ."

She flushed in the darkness. "I'm sorry, Father," she said. "I didn't mean . . ."

But Father Deener wasn't paying attention. He had suddenly remembered that he would have to report to the Bishop. Poor Rowdy, he thought: he'll have to come, after all.

"One must pay," he said aloud, "to ransom man from his own stupidity; and those into whose hands has been placed his salvation must pay the most."

"Yes," said Mary, not realizing that he had been talking to himself. "Yes . . . if I do really love him . . ."

I would give anything in the world to save Alfred, she thought sadly, but I have nothing.

"The shepherd," Father Deener continued, talking to himself, "cannot hold back. Whoever loves, must guard, and give of himself without stint. 'For God so loved mankind that He sent His only-begotten Son into the world that we might live through Him.'

" 'Where your treasure is,' " he said, " 'there will your heart be also.' "

"My heart," said Mary. "Yes."

Clasping her hands together, she lifted her face

to the night-blue sky. "Oh," she breathed; "would he take mine instead, as ransom?"

"What are you saying?" cried Father Deener in alarm. "Hush, my child; he might hear you!"

"But I want him to hear me!" exclaimed Mary. And just as Alfred had offered his soul for Gladys Milhouser, she too cried out to the darkness:

"Take my heart instead of his!"

Above them in the town the lights suddenly winked out, and the earth shook, and Mrs. Fleming, playing a game of solitaire with herself, was caught in the dark just as she was about to cheat with a red eight on a red nine. The room rocked a little, and the lights went on again, and Mrs. Fleming hastily put the red eight in the discard where it belonged. "There'll be some calls," she said to her husband, the doctor; "you'd better be sure your bag is ready. You'll need your stethoscope; I washed it in alcohol before supper. You'll find it in the bathroom."

Since no one was watching, she put the red eight

back on the red nine again. "Things haven't been the same since that new man moved in," she declared.

Sally Ewart and Henry Muggins, lying together in the porch swing at Sally's house, stared at each other in wonder. "Did you feel the earth rock, Sally?" Henry asked; and Sally replied with shining eyes:

"It was like Hemingway!"

Only Alfred, sitting alone in his little room above the shop, failed to notice anything out of the ordinary. His heart was so empty; all the world was empty, like his heart. Somewhere there was a memory of something—a fragrance, a woman's arms, soft fingers in his hair . . . it was beautiful and sad and like homesickness. But even that was faint, and growing fainter. If he thought about Gladys Milhouser at all, it was with a sort of wonder: had he really wanted her? But why?

He wanted nothing. Except to lay his head on Mary's lap again. . . .

Gladys slept through the shaking of the earth, and dreamed of swans. They were white and beautiful, but when she went to pet them they hissed at her. One of them turned into Dr. Hod, and brought her a cup of water. As she held it, he bent and kissed her. "It is from a stranger," he said; when she tasted it, it was as bitter as tears. She held out her arms to him, but he turned away; she saw that he had become a snake, and she set her heel on his head.

She woke up crying. High above the house in the cold, blue light of dawn, Beelzebub flew west toward the retreating night. To fishermen on the shore he looked like an enormous swan.

Mr. Oates, the pharmacist, smelled brimstone in the air, and fixed himself a gargle of Listerine and hot water. But Miss Olney spent the night in a closet. She was growing used to it.

CHAPTER 19

Early next morning, after matins, Samael went to
seek Father Deener in the church. He found the
priest standing in front of the statue of the great
Archangel, with a thoughtful and not entirely un-
critical expression on his face. Surprised to see his
adversary of the night before, and amazed to find
a demon in his church, Father Deener pointed to
St. Michael, and remarked ruefully:

"He does not look so invincible today."

"Your artist," said Samael, gazing up at the statue, "has pictured him as a milksop. I assure you, Father, he is nothing of the kind; you should have seen him when, at the head of his angels, he overthrew our legions. Even Lucifer looked gentle beside him, and paled in comparison.

"But you—you also look pale, my friend; did you not have a comfortable night?"

"No," said Father Deener. "I slept poorly. That is one thing a loser can count on: an uncomfortable night."

Samael regarded him quizzically. "A loser?" he remarked; "I am not so sure." And going to the stoup of holy water, he dipped his fingers into it.

Father Deener's eyes almost popped out of their sockets. Scarcely able to breathe from fright, he fell to his knees, and lifting his arms to Heaven, commanded:

"Smite him, Lord!"

Samael gently helped him to his feet. "You misunderstood me, Father," he said. "That was not a gesture of defiance, but rather a mark of reverence."

And as the priest gazed at him in astonishment, he went on: "We who were once His beloved children are not afraid to give praise to the Most High. We give credit to the Creator of life, which is very valuable as a witness both to Heaven and Hell."

"Life is not valuable without love," said Father Deener. And he added earnestly:

"It is the only link we have to Heaven."

The demon was silent, contemplating the church with its altar, above which a stained-glass window depicted an angel in the act of transfixing a serpent with his spear. "I have thought a great deal about love," he said presently, "and I have seen many examples of it. But lately I witnessed two actions which made a deep impression on me. Last night, on the sands of the shore, witnessed by the breaking waves, a woman no longer young and beautiful offered her heart for the life of the man she loved. Her heart was her life, it was all she had. 'Greater love hath no man than this, that he should lay down his life for his friend."

"The Devil," said Father Deener bleakly, "can quote Scripture for his own purposes."

For a moment Samael's eyes blazed with anger, lighting the small church with a blue flame. "You are a fool!" he exclaimed. "I was touched by your innocence, but I can see that your ignorance is as great as that of a beetle or an ant."

"With this difference," replied Father Deener stoutly: "that a bettle's ignorance leads him only to fear, whereas mine leads me to faith."

Samael made a resigned gesture. "After all," he said, "I didn't come here to quarrel with you. Forgive me for losing my temper: I always make the same mistake of expecting to be understood before I have even explained myself. . . ."

Seating himself on the edge of a pew, he clasped his knee in his hands and swung his foot to and fro. "I know that you love God," he said, "and that you have never seen Him. That is a somewhat mystical love, is it not? I should not wish to disparage it, or question your right to love what— or whom—you please, but it has occurred to me that you might have room in your heart for something more. Do you know what else I saw last night? I saw that you loved mankind: that you loved man, even with all the evil that is in him; and I thought . . . I thought . . .

"I thought that you might even be able to love me," he got out at last with difficulty, "although I know you do not think so."

Father Deener was so astonished that at first he was unable to reply. He was amazed, shocked, and mortified; and filled with indignation. But after a while he began to wonder if there might not be some justice in what Samael said. For we are told to hate evil, he thought, and yet it is true that I love mankind. I see in man much that is evil, much that is dark and sorrowful, and yet I do not hate him; on the contrary, my heart is full of pity for him. It took the demon to point this out to me.

Nevertheless, he too, in this world which no human mind has ever been able to understand, must go about the business to which he has been assigned. He is also one of God's creatures, of darkness rather than light; and God has not loved him for a long time.

It would be presumptuous of me to oppose God's unalterable law.

And turning to Lucifer's emissary, he said gently:

"It is out of the question."

"You cannot love me at all?" asked Samael unhappily.

Father Deener shook his head. "I am only little," he said. "I do not make the rules. Anathema you are, and must remain. I am sorry for you."

"I have no use for your pity," said Samael. And he rose slowly from the pew.

"I do not know anything about that," said Father Deener with energy, "but it is the best I can do.

And in exchange I must insist that you give up all thought of taking Miss Sebastian back with you. You cannot have her, no matter how willing she is to sacrifice herself."

Samael smiled sadly. "Don't worry, Father," he said, "we are not without some knowledge of history. Such a sacrifice, so innocent, so guileless, would certainly be considered a basis for sainthood; and we would have her only to lose her again. Her soul would be in Heaven, and since heart and soul are mystically but closely joined in the spirit, we should be constantly embarrassed as each clamored to be reunited with the other. No, Father—your friend is safe from me. When she offered herself last night, I received an electric shock which has lasted until today in the form of a headache."

"And Alfred?" asked Father Deener, taking hope.

Samael shrugged his shoulders. "Actually," he said, "his heart is so small that it is scarcely worth the trouble. I am leaving it behind in Miss Sebastian's care. Perhaps she will be able to enlarge it during the course of their life together.

"As for me," he went on, "I do not complain. It has been an interesting experience, on the whole. Indeed, at one point . . ." He hesitated and even appeared for a moment to be slightly embarrassed. "To tell you the truth, Father," he confided, "I found Miss Milhouser . . . Gladys . . . rather too much for me."

He held up his hand to show that he was not yet finished. "Please do not misunderstand," he said: "I was not given the shape of men's baser appetites for nothing. But at the same time, I have not been used to having to defend myself."

"Good heavens!" ejaculated Father Deener. "From Miss Milhouser?"

"Not directly, perhaps," said Samael a little sheepishly. "But something frightened me."

Father Deener nodded thoughtfully. "There are new ideas abroad," he declared, "and new ways, and a fresh wind over the old places. I do not know if it is good or bad, this generation which is so different from my own. So many of these young women who are so free and outspoken and give themselves to love so lightly, nevertheless marry early and raise large families. They are already faithful wives and excellent mothers at an age when the women of my generation were still mostly sighing for the moon."

"I knew that generation," said Samael with relish: "corseted in whalebone, shaped like an hourglass, laced and ruffled to the . . ."

Father Deener closed his eyes in pain. "Please," he begged: "respect my cloth!"

The demon made a gesture of apology. "Forgive me, Father," he murmured; "I forgot myself. These winds of change, as you call them, often cause me to feel a chill, and I warm myself at my memories. I have always had a weakness for the nineteenth century, and when at home I often visit Mademoiselle Duplessis in the Second Circle, and we exchange stories and anecdotes in French."

He paused, considering. "I do not think that Gladys . . . Miss Milhouser . . . would fit into any of the circles," he said, "but I have left her a memory of sorrow and delight which should help to make a good wife and mother of her someday, although her husband will never know what makes her smile now and then in her sleep, or wake with tears on her eyelids. He will think it is himself: it is the only revenge I shall take on him.

"And so, goodbye, Father. It is a long goodbye, for I shall never see you again, until the final trump, when all is forgiven. And even then we will have to wave to each other, across the abyss. I could wish that I was going home with a little more to show for my efforts, but it will not be the first time that we have lost a contract in escrow."

He turned slowly, wiping the last drops of moisture from his hand with his handkerchief. "In any case," he said cheerfully, "there are always the ants."

And with an enigmatic smile, he left the church.

Early sunlight lay over Parish, and long, blue-black shadows stretched themselves across the grass still white with dew. In the doorway of the Funeral Parlor, Mr. Venner sniffed the air, fresh and cold from the sea. The bell of the morning Angelus pealed out above the streets and houses, and floated off above the hills.

Mr. Venner thought he had never heard it sound so clear and sweet before.

BOOKS BY

ROBERT NATHAN

Novels

THE DEVIL WITH LOVE (1963)   A STAR IN THE WIND (1962)
THE WILDERNESS-STONE (1961)
THE COLOR OF EVENING (1960)   SO LOVE RETURNS (1958)
THE RANCHO OF THE LITTLE LOVES (1956)
SIR HENRY (1955)   THE TRAIN IN THE MEADOW (1953)
THE INNOCENT EVE (1951)   THE MARRIED LOOK (1950)
THE ADVENTURES OF TAPIOLA (1950)
(containing JOURNEY OF TAPIOLA, 1938,
and TAPIOLA'S BRAVE REGIMENT, 1941)
THE RIVER JOURNEY (1949)   LONG AFTER SUMMER (1948)
MR. WHITTLE AND THE MORNING STAR (1947)
BUT GENTLY DAY (1943)   THE SEA-GULL CRY (1942)
THEY WENT ON TOGETHER (1941)
PORTRAIT OF JENNIE (1940)   WINTER IN APRIL (1938)
THE BARLY FIELDS (1938)
(containing THE FIDDLER IN BARLY, 1926,
THE WOODCUTTER'S HOUSE, 1927,
THE BISHOP'S WIFE, 1928,
THE ORCHID, 1931, and THERE IS ANOTHER HEAVEN, 1929)
THE ENCHANTED VOYAGE (1936)   ROAD OF AGES (1935)
ONE MORE SPRING (1933)   JONAH (1925)

Poems

THE MARRIED MAN (1962)   THE GREEN LEAF (1950)
THE DARKENING MEADOWS (1945)
MORNING IN IOWA (1944)   DUNKIRK (1941)
A WINTER TIDE (1940)   SELECTED POEMS (1935)

Theater

JEZEBEL'S HUSBAND & THE SLEEPING BEAUTY (*1953*)

For Young People

THE SNOWFLAKE AND THE STARFISH (*1959*)

Archaeology

THE WEANS (*1960*)

These are BORZOI BOOKS, *published in New York*
by ALFRED A. KNOPF

A NOTE ON THE TYPE

THE TEXT of this book is set in CALEDONIA, a Lino-
type face designed by W. A. Dwiggins (1880-
1956), the man responsible for so much that is
good in contemporary book design and typography.
Caledonia belongs to the family of printing types
called "modern face" by printers—a term used to
mark the change in style of type-letters that occurred about 1800. Caledonia borders on the gen-
eral design of Scotch Modern but is more freely
drawn than that letter.

Composed, printed, and bound by
H. Wolff, New York.
The binding is based on an original design by
W. A. DWIGGINS